The Stress File

The Stress File

Editor

Colm Keane

RTÉ

Published in association with
Radio Telefís Éireann

BLACKWATER PRESS

Editor
Rosemary Dawson

Design and Layout
Liz Murphy

ISBN 0 86121 853 1

© 1997 The Contributors

Produced and printed in Ireland by
Blackwater Press,
7/8 Broomhill Business Park,
Tallaght, Dublin 24.

British Library Cataloguing-in-Publication Data.
A catalogue record is available.

Contents

List of Contributors

Colm Keane, Senior Producer, Radio Telefís Éireann.

Anthony Clare, Medical Director, St Patrick's Hospital, Dublin; Clinical Professor of Psychiatry, Trinity College, Dublin.

Anthony Bates, Senior Clinical Psychologist, St James's Hospital, Dublin.

Marie Murray, Principal Clinical Psychologist, St Vincent's Psychiatric Hospital and St Joseph's Adolescent Services, Dublin.

Myra Doherty, Behavioural Psychotherapist, Sligo-Leitrim Mental Health Services, North-Western Health Board.

John Griffin, Consultant Psychiatrist and Director of the Eating Disorders Programme, St Patrick's Hospital, Dublin.

John Sheehan, Consultant in Liaison Psychiatry, Mater Hospital, Dublin and Rotunda Hospital, Dublin.

Yvonne Tone, Senior Behavioural Psychotherapist, St Patrick's Hospital, Dublin.

Rolande Anderson, Assistant Director, Alcohol-Chemical Dependence Programme, St Patrick's Hospital, Dublin.

Elizabeth Lawlor, Clinical Psychologist, St John of God Hospital, Stillorgan, Co. Dublin.

Ann Marie McMahon, Counselling Psychologist, St John of God Hospital, Stillorgan, Co. Dublin.

Gerard Butcher, Cognitive Behavioural Psychotherapist, St John of God Hospital, Stillorgan, Co. Dublin.

Miriam Moore, Clinical Psychologist and Consultant in Pain Management, St Vincent's Hospital, Dublin.

Shane Hill, Programme Manager, The Cluain Mhuire Psychiatric Community Service, Blackrock, Co. Dublin.

Margo Wrigley, Consultant Psychiatrist in The Psychiatry of Old Age, Eastern Health Board and Mater Hospital, Dublin.

Tom Moriarty, Senior Clinical Psychologist, St John of God Hospital, Stillorgan, Co. Dublin.

Introduction

by

Colm Keane

Anxiety, tension, irritability, agitation, restlessness, tiredness, head-ache, poor appetite, loss of sleep and lack of energy are just some of the symptoms of stress.

These may be accompanied by panic, sweating, trembling hands, shortness of breath, tightness in the chest, irrational fears, depression, despair and a general feeling that life is out of control.

The symptoms may result from many factors including bereave-ment, separation, loneliness, boredom, marriage, pregnancy, illness, shock, financial strain, work problems or from an inability to cope with the pressures of everyday life.

They may cause or contribute to excessive alcohol consumption, smoking, ulcers, skin rashes, menstrual problems, heart attacks, certain forms of cancer, hypertension, asthma and a wide range of psychological disorders.

If you feel you have any of these symptoms of stress, you may well need help. If so, this book – a companion to the RTE Radio 1 series of the same name – will offer you information, advice and a strategy to get your life back together again.

The Stress File series on RTE Radio 1, together with this publication, set out to examine the causes, consequences and manifestations of stress in Ireland today. 'Stress is what we experience when there is a significant lack of balance between the resources we possess and the demands made upon us', says Professor Anthony Clare in his opening chapter. This theme is continued by Dr John Sheehan: 'When too much stress occurs, a person begins to feel that he is running just to keep still. A sense of being overloaded occurs and the person's performance begins to drop off.'

But what are the key causes of stress that can result in such devastating effects to the sufferer? Shyness, or *social phobia*, a common problem which severely affects at least one out of every twenty in our population, is identified by Dr Anthony Bates. 'If untreated, the duration of this problem can be lifelong, and one in every two sufferers will develop secondary problems such as depression, alcohol addiction and marital breakdown', he says.

Then there is *personal isolation* caused by loss, loneliness, shame, retirement, stigma or just simply by being different from everyone else. 'Loss, loneliness and personal isolation are all very closely interconnected', says Dr Ann Marie McMahon. 'They result in the fear that nothing will ever change and that you will never be able to enjoy yourself as you did in the past'.

Stresses at *work* caused by poor pay, bad working conditions, lack of recognition and uncertainties about permanence are examined by Gerard Butcher. 'If any, or indeed more than just one, of the items on this list apply to you, it would not be surprising if you felt under stress', he comments.

Nor is it surprising to hear of the stresses linked to diet and food, particularly given the social stigma attached to obesity. 'Stress caused by *eating disorders*, whether they be anorexia nervosa, bulimia nervosa, binge eating disorders, compulsive overeating or comfort eating should not be underestimated', Dr John Griffin concludes.

The chapters in this book also examine the stresses of age, especially those acquired in *adolescence* and in the process of growing old. Marie Murray talks about the one in five adolescents who experience what is called 'storm and strife' and the one in ten who will go on to experience a real crisis. 'Change always involves an element of stress and such vast changes therefore bring a vast array of stresses', she says.

Dr Margo Wrigley refers to the vulnerability of *old age*, the loss of health, mobility and independence, the isolation, the lack of finance and the loss of work, friends and relatives. 'Some old people are prey to stress and suffer greatly', she says. 'Crippling poor self-esteem may result, with older people feeling they have no role in society and are without value'.

Continuing with the issue of age, the ever-growing incidence of incest and child sexual abuse is examined by Dr Miriam Moore who reports: 'Many of these children will develop *PTSD (Post-Traumatic Stress Disorder)* and will be left with deep psychological wounds that do not heal but continue to fester and pour forth their poison way beyond childhood'.

Likewise, Shane Hill examines *schizophrenia*, which affects one in every hundred, especially those between the ages of 16–25. 'As the sufferer is losing the control of his mind under a sea of terrifying thoughts and becoming more isolated from his family and society in general, the families are at a complete loss as to how to understand or explain what is happening', he concludes.

Whatever the causes, the consequences of stress can be alarming. For a start, there is *chronic fatigue*. 'Chronic fatigue is a stressful condition ... those affected often feel misunderstood by others or find their illness may not be taken seriously', says Yvonne Tone.

Then there is *migraine*, with its uniquely excruciating, pulsating pain affecting one in every twelve of our population. 'A considerable literature expounds the large number of sufferers, the high cost to the person in question and society, and the often crushing effects it has on personal and family life', according to Elizabeth Lawlor.

Nor can we forget *alcohol dependence*, with anywhere from 6–18% of drinkers destined to become alcoholics. 'For those who are dependent on alcohol, alcohol only adds to the stresses of everyday life and can ultimately destroy their very existence', says Rolande Anderson.

Above all, this book offers hope for sufferers of stress. Despite commonplace feelings of helplessness, hopelessness and despair, stress *is* treatable, says Myra Doherty. Referring to the treatment of *panic*, she points out that success rates are as high as 80–90%. 'It is relatively easy to treat, with patience, understanding and education', she says.

Finally, Tom Moriarty lists the *stress management* strategies, the role of positive thinking and relaxation techniques and concludes: 'There is no doubt that you can be far more effective in the way you deal with stress providing you make the decision to do something about it. Take courage from the fact that others who have made this decision have been extremely successful in coping.'

There are many people to be thanked for their help in compiling this book. In particular, my thanks to the contributors and to the people who openly and honestly spoke about their anxieties on *The Stress File* programme on RTE Radio 1. My gratitude to Professor Anthony Clare for his continued encouragement. I would also like to mention Michael Littleton, Paddy Glackin and Kevin Healy, of RTE, who backed the idea. Finally, my thanks to Úna O'Hagan and Seán Keane who supported me through the many months of research into what has been, I hope, a worthwhile and valuable project.

Colm Keane.

What is Stress?

by

Professor Anthony Clare

One of the problems about stress is that while it is clearly regarded as an important issue it is not always clear what the word *Stress* is supposed to mean. Sometimes, we use stress to refer to the person, situation or event that causes us to feel bad and out of control. So we refer to a relative who is very demanding or an employment situation or to heavy traffic as *Stress*. In fact, it is more accurate to refer to such possible causes as *Stressors*. Sometimes, we use it to refer to the physical and psychological changes that occur in situations that appear stressful – such as our heart beating faster or the sweating or the feelings of fear and panic. Then again, we describe as stress the actual physiological changes which may occur in a stressed body – the elevations in the hormone level, adrenaline, the excess production of gastric juice, the increased physical tension in our chest and limb muscles.

Definitions of stress, particularly specialist ones, do not always help either. For example, according to the highly respected *Oxford Textbook of Medicine*, stress is 'the totality of the physiological reaction to an adverse or threatening stimulus itself'. Another definition describes stress as 'any force that puts a psychological or physical factor beyond its range of stability, producing a strain within the individual. Knowledge that a stress is likely to occur constitutes a threat to the individual. A threat can cause a strain because of what it signifies to the individual'. A less technical and more readily comprehensible definition is that stress is what we experience when there is a significant lack of balance between the resources we possess and the demands made upon us.

Conventional wisdom suggests that we become stressed when too much is asked of us and so we feel unable to cope and feel out of control. But less recognised is the fact that a significant lack of balance can also occur if not enough is demanded of someone, if demand does not match resources – as happens, for example, to the unemployed, to people working below their capacity and to people capable of giving much more than is asked of them. It is not sufficiently appreciated that boredom, a lack of stimulation, can be very stressful.

Whatever the cause – excessive or inadequate demand, inappropriate or deficient resources – stress is common. But a certain degree of stress is not only harmless, it is probably to be welcomed. Human beings appear to desire a degree of stress and indeed to actively seek it. We take risks, test ourselves, put ourselves in situations, be it in sports or work, in which we will be stressed. A few nerves before an important meeting or performance can be positively helpful. Everybody needs a certain amount of stress to be alert and healthy. The problem arises when the feeling of demand, the challenge, the stimulation is accompanied by a sense of loss of control, a sense that the stress is mastering us instead of us mastering the stress. Long-term excessive stress is harmful, escalates the process of 'wear and tear' on the body and leads to a variety of psychological and physical disorders.

It could be argued that the key feature of pathological stress is the feeling of losing control, of impending disintegration, of sheer panic. Brian, a businessman in his 30s, who set up on his own and then began to find the pressure difficult to cope with, describes it graphically:

> *'I reckon it was the lowest point of my life. Beyond a shadow of a doubt it really was. I felt terrible. I began to feel I wasn't in control of my life and, more, that something else was controlling me. I could feel an impending doom and it was getting progressively worse.'*

In many instances, the Brians of this world are being controlled by something else, by something outside them, be it the demands of the job or the expectations of society. People under stress struggle to regain control while often concealing even from their nearest and dearest just how precarious and on the verge of breakdown they feel. Indeed, the sheer effort of trying to convince everyone else that you are coping can actually worsen the stress. Here is Kate, a woman in her 20s, who following the death of her mother from Multiple Sclerosis developed the conviction that she herself had the disease:

> *'I felt everybody was relying on me, draining on me, leaning on me ... I was keeping the house, keeping my boyfriend happy, trying to be the life and soul of the party with my friends ... and this was draining on me all the time, sapping my energy and there was nothing left for me.'*

The key physical symptoms of stress include palpitations, churning of the stomach, sweating, dry mouth, dizziness, irritability, sleep disturbance and muscle tension. Sometimes, the symptoms are so dramatic and frightening that sufferers from stress become preoccupied with the possibility that they have some life-threatening physical disease such as heart disease or cancer. Kate thought she might have an illness like multiple sclerosis, not merely because her mother had suffered from it and many of the symptoms seemed similar but because she herself was experiencing puzzling physical symptoms:

> *'I had tingling in the fingers, some fingers went numb. I was very sensitive to light and noise. My balance was very much affected. Also my coordination – I was bumping into people or not avoiding things on time, like dustbins or lampposts ... I decided I definitely had multiple sclerosis and the more I thought about it the worse the symptoms became.'*

Indeed, one of the major problems in helping people tackle stress is that many sufferers find it very difficult indeed to accept that physical symptoms can be due to something such as stress. Proper physical examination, together with a full account of the development of the symptoms, usually makes plain what is actually happening. Providing an explanation of what happens to the body when it is exposed to stress usually reassures the stress sufferer.

The commonest psychological symptom of stress is an impending sense of collapse or doom. In addition, there is irritability, indecisiveness, a loss of concentration and drive, and intense and paralysing panic. Not surprisingly, if the stress persists, the affected individual can become quite depressed. Andrew, a successful businessman in his 20s, who began to experience severe stress, describes the way it happens:

> *'It's like feeling completely alone and isolated. It's like feeling that no matter where you are, what you're doing, you just want to lie down and pull the covers over you. I had this feeling that everything around me, time and space, would stop and I could step outside ... I felt I couldn't cope with things any more ... It was a very lonely time. Depression is a very lonely thing. Although you are supported by family and friends, at the end of the day you're the one who wakes up in the morning feeling totally depressed and wondering is this going to get better?'*

Almost anything can be either a resource to help ease stress or a demand causing or exacerbating it. Take, for example, a marital relationship or a family network. For some, a successful, supportive, harmonious marriage can provide a robust buffer to keep the negative effects of, say, a stressful job at bay. For others, it may well be the marriage itself that is the stress. Over 20 years ago, two American researchers constructed what they called 'a social readjustment scale' which attempted to quantify the stress involved in negotiating different life changes. At the top of the list, what research appeared to indicate to be the most stressful experience, was death of a spouse. Other particularly stressful life changes include marital separation and divorce, marriage itself, being fired from work, retirement, pregnancy, the death of a sibling or close friend and a son or daughter leaving school. Common to many of these stresses is isolation – the loneliness which follows death, divorce or children leaving home and the difficulty of imagining a full and satisfying life ever again. Michael, a college-educated business executive who became unemployed at the age of 42, describes the stresses:

> *'I couldn't see a future. I absolutely could not see a future. I would have been at the peak of what I was doing in the company I worked in. Now, all of a sudden, I was virtually on the scrap heap ... more than anything else, I couldn't see a future and it was a very bleak outlook.'*

The importance of isolation in the genesis of stress-related illness was illustrated in a famous study of heart attacks carried out in

Alameda County in California and reported first in 1979. Over 4,000 individuals were followed up over nine years. The researchers controlled for such complicating factors as smoking, obesity, high blood pressure and family history, factors that are already well-known to be implicated in the causation of heart disease. They then found that those individuals who were classified as socially isolated on a very reliable research measure were two and a half times more likely to suffer a heart attack than those individuals judged to have good social networks. Put another way, a most important protection against stress and stress-related diseases is social integration; being part of a network; being a valued and integrated member of a community.

The nature and the demands of modern society often militate against healthy living. Many working people find themselves caught up in a work cycle that leaves little room for relaxation and leisure. Many women find themselves struggling to match the demands of work and child-rearing. Many nuclear families are now incapable of providing the kind of mutual support that was a feature of the extended family of a generation ago. Yet, the message from stress research is clear. The road back from a breakdown due to excessive stress starts with the acknowledgement that the individual is not an island but needs and benefits from the understanding and the support of others. Indeed, Michael, the business executive quoted above, regards this as a lesson he has learned as a result of becoming unemployed:

> *'It has taught me to appreciate family and friends an awful lot more than I did before, and how valuable they are, particularly my father with whom I hadn't a great relationship ... You do find there are people who actually care.'*

If the experience of losing control is a cardinal feature of severe stress, the sense of gaining it is part and parcel of recovery. Take the issue of guilt. Many people, particularly those who are depressed or whose self-esteem is seriously damaged or who, having suffered a particular trauma, find that they are blaming themselves for their predicament, experience a crushing guilt. People who have been sexually abused feel guilt. People who have been mugged in the street feel guilty. People who have been fired from their jobs through no fault of their own, nevertheless often find themselves irrationally concluding that they are, in fact, to blame. The stress of the initial traumatic event is compounded by the guilt that follows. But as Jane who suffered for over 30 years from stress-related anxiety and depression points out, you need to recognise where your responsibility for something starts and stops:

> *'Set your boundaries because that's the only way you can get rid of the guilt. Your limits are there and nobody can tell you what is not right. You have your boundaries and no one can cross them, neither your kids, your husband, nor your mum and dad – nobody should cross that boundary ... and if we could cut the guilt out of our lives an enormous amount of the stress could go.'*

That is not to say that there is no such thing as healthy guilt, there is. But such guilt involves the recognition that something needs to be done other than just experiencing and re-experiencing the guilt. Unworked-through guilt, guilt without forgiveness and an attempt at recompense are other classic examples of a demand without a matching response.

Recovery involves facing and eliminating guilt. In turn, this means taking a greater responsibility for and control of your life. But even here there needs to be caution. Some people experience stress because they take too much on, they need to do everything, to be indispensable and absolutely self-reliant. They feel guilty if they call upon others to share the load. Their lack of confidence and self-esteem is masked by an inordinate desire to serve, to provide and to meet other people's needs. Helping such people regain control and relieve their stress involves persuading them to recognise what it is they are doing. Here is Brian again, reflecting on how he began to set his stressful business life to rights:

> *'I had to realise that I had to let them have the responsibility and not try and take everything on myself. I had to learn to trust people again to a certain degree ... I've learned to plan better, to set goals and objectives which were things I heard of but never really did.'*

Of course, some of the remedies that stressed people use to bring about relief contribute to the confusion and worsen the symptoms. One common response is for the individual under stress to drink more alcohol in order to dampen down the distressing feelings of tension and panic. Alcohol, in the initial stages, eases tension. The problem is that this effect is short-lived. For Ruairi, a young alcoholic in his 20s, alcohol seemed the remedy for the exceedingly unpleasant tension he was routinely feeling:

> *'Your mind,' he said of his feelings of stress, 'is racing constantly. You are panicking. You are paranoid. There is terrible indecision even regarding the simplest things. There's complete apathy, you just want to hide away, you just want to drown yourself in a way, you know.'*

Like many others before and since, Ruairi ended up drowning himself in alcohol and then the remedy for his stress ended up as its major cause:

> *'The principle stress, I suppose, is needing a drink, needing the lubricant to talk to people, needing it to be over the edge before you can communicate with people ... you need to be drunk, basically, and once that is reached, once you are in your own mind communicating with people, you're on your way. Then, that's it, that's goodnight.'*

Ruairi's experience neatly illustrates how something that appears to help in the relief of stress ends up aggravating it, in this case alcohol. Other 'crutches' to which people turn include smoking, tranquillisers, illicit drugs, and gambling.

There are some very basic rules concerning the avoidance of stress. First, there is the necessity of getting your priorities right. Potential sources of stress should be noted; at home, at work, in your personal and social life. The important thing is to be in control rather than at the mercy of your environment. People who manage stress, manage their lives. They learn to delegate appropriately. They learn to say *No* rather than taking on more than they can cope with. There is the necessity of knowing what you can and cannot do, and where the boundaries of your and other people's responsibilities lie. Karen, who once was so stressed she suffered from crippling migraine, sums up the importance of taking control:

> *'You have to take responsibility for your own actions. You cannot be responsible for how other people behave, you don't have power over how they behave. Likewise, if*

you think positively about a situation, and not just think about it but truly believe it, this will have a very healthy affect on the mind and body ... conversely, if you have negative thoughts and energy – like "I can't do that, I should do that, I ought to do that", you'll have negative energy and you won't get very far.'

It also helps to stop smoking, modify drinking and learn some basic relaxation techniques. More serious symptoms of stress may require specialised cognitive therapy aimed at changing attitudes and modifying stressful behaviour. These days, the use of drugs to relieve stress is less popular. There is widespread recognition that many of the drugs widely used in the 1960s and 1970s to reduce anxiety and ease stress were addictive. Now, minor tranquillisers are usually only used in acutely stressful states to relieve distress. Another group of drugs, the selective serotonin re-uptake inhibitors (SSRIs), of which fluoxetine (PROZAC) is the first and best-known, has been found to be helpful in the treatment of panic attacks.

In summary, these days no one should suffer severe stress without recognising what is happening and knowing what to do to achieve relief. The signs and symptoms of stress are neither mystifying nor rare. We all know what it is like to feel stressed, panicky, tense and potentially out of control. Now, there are simple steps which can be taken to avert stress and systematic approaches to control and relieve stress when it occurs.

2

Social Phobia

by

Dr Anthony Bates

When I was in my second year in university, my class seemed to be divided into two types of people, those who were outgoing and confident, and those who were shy and insecure. The first group appeared to the rest of us not to have a care in the world. They spoke out in class, they made jokes, laughed, and they seemed to get along very easily with everybody. The rest of the class, including myself, were less sure of ourselves. We felt awkward if a lecturer addressed a question to us, and we found it difficult to strike up a conversation with students we didn't know. Of course, we never admitted our nervousness to anyone. We simply kept to ourselves and tried hard to 'look cool'. Then something happened which made me see my classmates in a new way, and realise something about people that I've never forgotten.

Someone brought a book into class which was passed around from one student to another. Written by John Powell, the book was entitled *Why am I afraid to tell you who I am?* It was a short book with a simple message, i.e. that all of us have our own particular fears and insecurities, and we find it really difficult to admit this to one another. We believe that if others know just how inadequate we feel sometimes, they will think of us as different, or odd in some way. The book was so sensitive and accurate in its account of this fear that, personally, I felt someone had been reading my most private thoughts and written them down. What amazed me, moreover, was how everyone who read it had the same reaction. Even those who appeared very confident admitted that this book seemed to describe them. As it got passed around, a conversation developed between us that broke down many barriers, and we realised we had more in common than we had ever believed possible. We each harboured our particular insecurities, whether they concerned our looks, our accent, our dress, or our intelligence. While we would reveal some parts of ourselves, we firmly believed others would reject us if they knew how inadequate we often felt inside. This book allowed us to be honest with one another, and as it weaved its way around the class it was like a ribbon that drew together people who had previously felt themselves to be quite separate.

It is probably safe to say that we have all felt this fear of other people at some stage of our lives. Maybe it was a general shyness of the kind described above, or perhaps something happened in specific situations with people that made us intensely anxious, and left us uneasy in the company of others for some time afterwards. We may have found ourselves blushing for no apparent reason and felt terrified that others would notice our discomfort and laugh at us. Or we may remember standing up to speak in front of others and been so overcome with tension that the speech we had planned so carefully came out all wrong.

Most of us recover from these distressing experiences and we become comfortable in social situations over time. Others, however, do not. They seem to become less and less comfortable in social situations and gradually avoid people as much as they can. We describe this excessive fear of others as *Social Phobia*. This chapter reviews what we know about this problem, why it persists in some people and not in others, and how it can be helped.

The recognition of social phobia as a distinct problem is quite recent. In the mid-1960s it was first described by a group of researchers in London as a feeling of anxiety that occurs while performing a specific task in which the individual believes that he or she will be subject to the scrutiny of others. For some time after this there was a debate as to whether this problem was really just a variation of *Panic Disorder*. This latter difficulty refers to sudden physical sensations of anxiety, which individuals mistakenly interpret as a sign that there is something seriously wrong with their physical health, (e.g. that they are about to have a heart attack). Alternatively, they become terrified that their anxiety attack means they are on the verge of a complete mental breakdown.

An individual with social phobia does experience panic attacks but their fear is not of 'going crazy' or dying, but of doing something that will cause other people to ridicule them, and leave them feeling humiliated or embarrassed.

Consider the example of Linda, a 30-year-old woman with two children, who had become increasingly socially phobic since her teens. When she came for help with this problem, she described an episode of panic she had the day before. This experience seemed to typify what had been happening to her on an almost daily basis. Some new neighbours had recently moved in beside her and her children had become quite friendly with theirs. As time went by, they invited her to drop in so they could get to know each other. Having made numerous attempts to turn them down, she realised she had to meet with them. This was her description of what happened:

> 'The whole time I was there I felt on edge. I thought that at any moment, I might have an anxiety attack, so I sat there feeling trapped, cornered, like there was no escape. When Mary went out to make coffee, and left me sitting there alone with her husband, I lost it completely. I started to feel incredibly anxious and worried about him seeing how messed up I was. I blushed, I babbled, and I noticed my heart really speeding up and my breathing also. I looked anywhere but at him and tried to hide my face and put as much distance between us as I could. I saw myself sitting there looking incredibly stupid, and I imagined the conversations they'd have about the psycho next door, after I left.'

Clearly, this was a most distressing experience for Linda, and afterwards she went home and berated herself for being so stupid and letting herself down as she did. She added it to a long list of similar episodes, and felt more hopeless than ever that she could not beat this problem.

Since the mid-1980s, social phobia has been accepted as a distinct form of anxiety. Various attempts have been made to establish how common this problem is in the population, and different estimates have been reported. Results indicate that about 5% of the population experience social phobia in their lifetime, but this may be an underestimate. Social phobia has been found to be the only anxiety in which men are represented in equal or greater numbers than women.

It typically has its onset in the mid-teens, sometimes following a severe humiliating experience, or it can originate earlier in childhood.

People whose phobia began in their teenage years often recall a number of experiences of being embarrassed in school, or at work, or being humiliated in some way in their family. Whatever happened, they found that these experiences completely shattered their confidence, and left them in dread of having to enter certain social situations where they might become the focus of attention. They became terrified of doing something wrong socially, of other people noticing their discomfort, and ridiculing them. Rather than getting better at coping around people, their fears persisted and even worsened. Over time, they avoided more and more situations where they might be noticed or found 'wanting' in some way. Their self-confidence dropped and they may have turned down important educational or career opportunities rather than risk the trauma of other people seeing through them, and rejecting them as being inferior or stupid. Their lives became constricted to a few people with whom they felt safe and their range of satisfactions narrowed, until, at some point, life seemed to have very little joy or purpose.

Social phobics frequently hold the belief that there is a right and a wrong way of behaving socially. They worry excessively before entering social situations and tend to rehearse, over and over, what they will say or do. As they are speaking to others, they monitor what they are saying to check that they are coming across appropriately. Being over-rehearsed, and overly self-conscious, they can come across as very stilted or rigid, and may give others the mistaken impression that they are cold or unfriendly.

Earlier approaches to helping people who were socially anxious put a lot of emphasis on teaching them social skills in the hope that this would improve their self-confidence. However, these treatments were generally unsuccessful. While it is now agreed that social phobics are less at ease, less spontaneous, and more self-conscious than others in social situations, the consensus among clinicians is that they are not socially unskilled, but inhibited by their symptoms in using these skills.

It is interesting to note that while the problem is usually apparent by the mid-to-late teens, the average age for seeking help with this problem is 30 years of age. The social phobic feels quite ashamed of their difficulty around people and he or she may be as reluctant to talk to a GP or a counsellor as to anyone else, for fear that their problem will be regarded as unimportant or just stupid. If untreated, the duration of this problem can be lifelong, and one in every two sufferers will develop secondary problems such as depression, alcohol addiction, and marital breakdown. Alcohol, for many sufferers, becomes the only way they feel they can face social situations, but this excessive reliance on alcohol can lead to addiction. Social phobia may well be missed as the primary problem for many alcoholics, and if recovery does not attend to their social fears, these individuals may very well relapse.

In treating other phobias it has been found helpful to encourage the individual to repeatedly confront his or her fears until their anxiety reduces and they discover their worst fears don't happen. So, for example, if someone is terrified by the thought of being in a confined space, they may well be encouraged to spend increasing amounts of time in an elevator, or in a small room with the door closed, until their anxiety disappears. Through this type of gradual 'exposure' to their particular fear, they realise they can handle the situation and their confidence in dealing with similar situations is dramatically increased.

If one were to apply this 'exposure' principle to the treatment of social phobia, one might think of creating opportunities for sufferers to meet people in a safe setting and thereby overcome their fears. This has been the main treatment approach used for this problem, but it has been singularly unsuccessful. For some reason, simply meeting people doesn't help the socially phobic person. When researchers considered this fact they realised that socially phobic individuals are probably meeting people in their everyday life several times a day – whether they wish to or not – and still their fears persist and worsen. Researchers in Oxford have tried to solve this puzzle. Why should social phobia be the one particular fear that doesn't reduce with exposure? They came up with two key insights:

Firstly, when a social phobic enters a threatening situation the focus of their attention shifts dramatically onto themselves. They become so preoccupied with a negative image of how they are coming across, that they actually fail to notice most of what is happening around them. Even if they are coming across quite well, in their own minds they see themselves as looking foolish, and they see others condemning them. In a very real way, it is not others who make them afraid, but rather the terrifying image they have of themselves when they are around people. Treatment must therefore give priority to changing this negative, distorted self-image.

Secondly, a characteristic of sufferers is that they develop specific strategies to make themselves feel safe in social situations where they feel under threat. Thus, the sufferer may take care to avoid eye-contact, to make sure that others don't see fear in their eyes. Or the individual who is afraid that others will notice that they sweat, may wear a vest and heavy coat to conceal this fact. They believe that by using these 'safety behaviours' they can prevent some feared catastrophe from occurring, such as someone realising they are anxious and making embarrassing comments about them.

These safety behaviours only make the situation worse: the person who constantly avoids eye-contact makes others feel uneasy, and the sufferer picks this up and becomes even more anxious; the individual who wears extra clothing to conceal perspiration actually perspires more, and as they feel this happening, they become more anxious. While safety behaviours seem obviously unhelpful, the socially phobic may hardly be aware that he or she is using them to control their anxiety. Even when they become aware of them, they may be convinced that these strategies are the only hope they have of coping with social encounters. Helping the sufferers identify their particular strategies and having them agree to 'drop' these behaviours and see what happens, has proved to be a great breakthrough in treating this condition.

What follows is a description of the most recent cognitive therapy approach to treating social phobia, developed in Oxford University, which has incorporated the key insights to understanding this condition, described above.

Cognitive therapy offers a systematic treatment based on the idea that how the social phobic thinks and behaves in a social situation is responsible for keeping them anxious. It works by first engaging the individual in a fact-finding mission to see what happens when they are troubled by anxiety attacks. Sufferers are encouraged to keep a careful diary of their reactions and write them down between sessions. By examining their reports a picture begins to emerge of what they are doing that might be keeping the problem alive. Some people discover that their anxiety is quite confined to specific social encounters, while for others it seems to happen in a much wider range of situations. Table 1 summarises a weekly diary returned by Linda, the 30-year-old woman mentioned earlier, who recorded key trigger situations for her anxiety, her symptoms and thoughts in these situations, and, finally, what she did to make herself feel safe in these situations, i.e. her safety behaviours.

Trigger situations	Physical symptoms	Negative thoughts	Safety behaviours
Meeting friend of one of my friends in a bar	Heart races rapidly	"*Oh my God*, this is awful"	Break eye contact Hunch shoulders
Sitting down talking to male friend face to face	Blushing	"I'm going to have a major panic attack"	Cover face
Somebody watching me intently doing something	Shaky voice	"How can I stop this person seeing what a basket case I am"	Smile a lot/talk a lot
Meeting someone I feel I might be attracted to sexually	Hot flushes	"If this guy thinks I'm sexually attracted to him, he'll think I'm a slut"	Curl up and make myself as insignificant as possible

Table 1: Typical social situations and reactions that characterised Linda's social phobia.

A common theme in Linda's accounts of her anxiety experiences was that of being in a situation where there was a potential for sexual attraction. She had grown up with a father who had berated her for appearing in any way 'sexual', and as a result, she was constantly alert to the danger of other people noticing signs of her sexuality. While she dressed to conceal rather than reveal her body, she feared that others would notice her and ridicule her as her father had done previously. Being in the company of a man triggered anxiety reactions which were sparked by negative thoughts such as, 'This guy will see I'm sexually attracted to him and think I'm a slut'. At other times she reported first becoming aware of unpleasant physical sensations, which were accompanied by thoughts such as, 'Oh my God, I'm going to panic ... this guy will see I'm a complete nutcase'. Physical sensations included shortness of breath, hot flushes, and a racing heart.

To cope with these crises she adopted certain safety behaviours. For example, she broke eye-contact, leaned away from the other person, hid her hands between her knees and partially covered her face. She believed these manoeuvres would reduce the chance her anxiety or her sexual interest would be detected. However, they only made her more aware of how anxious she was feeling, which in turn made her more convinced she was coming across as a 'nutcase', which in turn made her feel more anxious, and so on.

To break the vicious cycle of negative thoughts, feelings and behaviour that characterise social phobia, the following strategies are critical:

(a) Develop a more realistic image of oneself in social situations.

(b) Learn to focus attention on others rather than on oneself.

(c) Risk some new behaviour in social situations.

(d) Examine underlying negative beliefs about oneself and others.

(a) Developing a more realistic image of oneself in social situations.

Self-esteem is normally very low in the individual with social phobia, and this becomes very evident when they describe the image of themselves that becomes activated in social situations. David was a General Practitioner who had a successful practice and who was deeply committed to his patients. In spite of this, he had a severe phobia of meeting others outside his surgery, especially his own medical colleagues, whom he believed would notice his nervousness, and regard this as a sign that he was an inadequate doctor who probably shouldn't be in practice.

To allow him to check out the very negative image he had of himself around people, we arranged that he would talk to a colleague of mine, who knew nothing about him or his difficulties. He agreed that I would video this interaction so that we could look at it together and assess how well, or how badly, he came across.

Initially, he chatted to this stranger, employing all his usual 'safety behaviours'. Thus, he talked all the time, asking the other person lots of questions to keep attention away from himself, and he spoke very quickly so as to avoid awkward silences. Later, we made a second video recording where David agreed not to use these safety strategies. Rather than get the other person to talk about themselves, he revealed to this person that he was a medical doctor, and described the problem that had required him to seek my help. David and I watched both recordings and he was quite surprised to realise that his negative image about how 'awful' he came across was completely untrue. Furthermore, he discovered that when he dropped his safety behaviours, he actually looked a lot more relaxed and friendly. In fact, he realised that those safety behaviours, which he relied on to hide his anxiety from others, made him look more uneasy, and made it difficult for others to relax in his company.

Watching the video of his conversation with a stranger proved to be a key moment in David's recovery. Whereas others had often reassured him that he looked perfectly fine in social situations, it was the opportunity for him to see for himself how much better he came across, compared to how he had pictured himself, that changed his negative self-image.

(b) Learning to focus attention on others rather than on oneself.

One of the ways socially phobic people remain anxious around other people is by focusing completely on their inner discomfort and their negative self-image, and almost forgetting to attend to other people in their company. When you are so inwardly focused on your personal reactions it is difficult to also pick up what is happening around you. Research has shown that the only evidence social phobics have for other people's negative view of them, is that they felt so badly that they were sure this must have been the case. For example; one young man who passed people waiting at a bus-stop could describe how everyone seemed to be looking at him in a funny way, even though he had his head down the whole time and had never once looked at the faces of any of those people.

Helping the social phobic to shift their attention onto others with whom they are speaking has two important benefits. Firstly, they realise that others are usually quite friendly, rather than judgmental. Secondly, shifting their attention away from themselves onto others reduces the amount of anxiety they experience in social situations.

(c) Risking some new behaviour in social situations.
Many sufferers believe that they can handle social situations, and keep their anxiety under control, if they don't draw too much attention to themselves. Therefore, they may make sure to say very little, to avoid offering a conflicting opinion in a discussion, or to hide some personal detail about their background. They firmly believe that if others find out more about them, or discover they have strong personal opinions, they will ridicule or reject them. As long as these beliefs remain unchecked, sufferers will continue to believe that there is something wrong with them which must never be disclosed. While no one would deny that we all have the right to keep certain personal information private, social phobics carry this much too far. At some point they need to take calculated risks to see if their worst fears really come true.

Philip was a computer programmer who had dyslexia. He was ashamed of this and hid it from everyone outside his immediate family. He felt it made him inferior and different to others. He never wrote a card or a letter to a friend for fear this weakness might be exposed and he would lose their respect. After some years of isolating himself from others, he became deeply depressed, and one New Year's Eve he came perilously close to ending his life with a drug overdose. During the treatment programme that followed we had a session which ended with my inviting Philip to reveal his 'secret' to someone and observe their reaction. He left with this homework assignment. The first person he met was an ex-girlfriend whom he had not seen for a number of years. They went out for a meal together and talked for hours about old times. At some stage he remembered his homework and confided in her that he had recently been getting help to come to terms with dyslexia. She listened carefully and then asked him whether this had anything to do with the abrupt way he ended their relationship four years before. Philip admitted that his fear of her finding out had been a major reason for the breakup. She described how hurt she had felt at the time, since his leaving had made no sense to her at all. Now, at least, she had some way of making sense of what happened and their relationship could be more honest and open.

There is probably very little we could share about our inadequacies that would be shocking to others, because as humans we have all known moments of shame, moments of failure, and we probably all have families with skeletons somewhere in their cupboard. By taking the risk to share ourselves more honestly with others, we discover that our openness invites them, in turn, to be open with us, and our relationship moves to a deeper and more satisfying level. For some social phobics this may mean sharing some personal information; for others it may mean risking being more assertive with others; and for others it may be they need to allow themselves to admit that they are anxious when this happens, rather than trying desperately to cover it up. For Philip, this risk proved to be well worth taking. Two years after the 'reunion' with his girlfriend described above, they were married!

(d) Examine underlying negative beliefs about oneself and others.

Part of any successful treatment of social phobia involves examining some beliefs sufferers may hold about themselves and the world, which maintain their anxiety rather than help them to be at ease with people. Many social phobics carry beliefs about themselves that seriously undermine their self-esteem. These self-doubts may reflect what they learned at home. For example, one young man's family constantly threatened to send him off to the 'loony bin' because he was weird, and one young woman was constantly compared to brothers and told she was stupid because she wasn't as quick at learning as they were. Many such comments are remembered long into adulthood and can make it very hard for social phobics to be open with others about their personal difficulties. They fear that if they admit to having a problem in their life it will seem to prove that what they were told as children is true – that there is something 'wrong' with them.

Many social phobics have also picked up rigid family rules about how they should behave around others if they are to be accepted. For example, some families believe that 'other people can't be trusted', or they hold the belief that 'we should never let people outside our family know what goes on inside the family'. If these rules are over-emphasised it may make it difficult for someone to trust others when they need help and support, long after they have left home. These and other beliefs need to be identified and examined in the treatment of social phobia to prevent relapse and to enable the individual to develop more trust in themselves and in others.

The above describes a new approach to treating social phobia. It is based on the idea that the problem is a vicious cycle of anxiety, with a number of key features keeping it alive. Unlike previous attempts to treat this problem that relied on exposure, relaxation training, and social skill training, this model of treatment focuses on changing the individual's self-image, helping them to drop their safety behaviours, and to examine beliefs about themselves and the world that keep them afraid of allowing anyone to get close. Breaking out of the cycle of social anxiety frees the person to be themselves, and to relate more honestly and intimately to others. While relationships may be a source of pain at times, they are also the gateway to what makes life most rewarding for each of us. To be cut off from such experiences is the tragedy of social phobia. The cognitive model of treatment is a welcome and promising development in terms of what therapists can now offer sufferers.

Adolescent Stress

by

Marie Murray

This chapter attempts to enter and explore the world of adolescents and the conditions and circumstances that may lead them to be stressed, frustrated or depressed. One of our difficulties as adults is that we must revisit our own pasts which can be painful and envisage the future, which is more theirs than ours. I believe that because this can be a nostalgic or difficult process, we sometimes avoid it, or we may filter and screen our memories into idyllic images. Because of this, adolescents can sometimes feel abandoned to the category of 'adolescence' with all their struggles and stresses attributed to that term and so dismissed as a phase. This is a complaint often made by young people. If we wish to understand adolescents we must understand the individuals, the child growing into adulthood and also understand ourselves and our interactions with them, our beliefs about them, our fear of and for them and our emotions when they encounter stress or cause it.

If we can remember our own adolescence we have some idea of the emotionalism of that time. Can we remember the volcanic spot erupting, the gangly uncontrollable body, the exquisite pain of first love, the emotional swing from uncontainable happiness to intense sadness? Can we remember both loving and hating our parents at the same time, wanting to be a child and wanting to be grown up, wanting to be both and not knowing what we want at all? Can we recapture the emotion of a piece of music, a poem, a new idea, a film? Do we recall being praised, the intensity of friendships, feeling on the brink of life, of love, of being actively adored and unceremoniously dumped, of hysterical joy and of unbearable misery? What of the fear of not being part of the crowd, of saying the wrong thing, of the blush deepening when we notice it, of not being asked to dance or being refused when asking? Can we remember being innocent and being accused, of thinking we looked wonderful until an adult smirked indulgently, of working hard and getting a 'D' from an admired teacher, of not understanding and pretending to, and of peering into the mirror and the future with equal despair?

What distinguishes *adolescent stress* from other life-cycle stresses is perhaps this range of emotions and sources of stress at one of the most vulnerable stages in life; the letting go of childhood and the taking on of adulthood. This is a difficult task. The changes during adolescence involve physical, sexual, psychological, educational, family, spiritual, intellectual, social and vocational change. Change always involves an element of stress and such vast changes therefore bring a vast array of stresses. Indeed, given the enormity of these changes all adolescents may be expected to experience some stress, which can be expected at any stage of life and is part of living. It is a credit to adolescents that the majority manages to get through this stage so well and so successfully. Approximately 20% of adolescents may experience what is called 'storm and strife'. Only around 10% come to real crisis and clinical attention for a variety of reasons and about 5% of those aged 12–18 years suffer depressive disorders. When they do so, they are remarkable by how well they enter into therapy and how well many return to coping, particularly if we support and respect them through it. What we always need to distinguish are the normal stresses of this time from the signals of serious distress that adolescents transmit, how to know and recognise these signals and how to attend to them.

The *physical stresses* of adolescence extend from the onset of puberty until full maturity and lie not so much in the fact of change but in the rate of change. Changes vary both between individuals and between boys and girls. Girls tend to enter the process earlier than boys. Some studies show that adolescent boys who mature earlier are typically better adjusted than late maturers and have higher status and interactions with peers. A late maturing boy may suffer feelings of inadequacy about his height, weight and stature. He may be called 'a weed', 'a wimp', or even 'a girl'. Think of the pain those comments inflict.

Early maturing girls may feel 'gross', 'monstrous', 'awkward' and 'embarrassed', particularly if their bodily changes are the cause for the innuendo or unwelcome advances that the child within them is unable to cope with. Adult remarks on the physical development of adolescents can be experienced by them as patronising, painful, embarrassing or even abusive. We are all sensitive to comments about our appearance. As adults we don't much like remarks on receding hairlines, appearance of wrinkles, changes from youth to ageing. Positive body-image is important to all of us.

The onset of eating disorders, which are signals of deep stress and distress, peak in adolescence and are more common in girls than boys. In adolescence, failure to develop a positive body image in addition to other life stresses can cause a shift from the usual adolescent dissatisfaction with appearance, weight and figure, to eating disorders such as dieting to starvation *(anorexia nervosa)* and gorging–purging *(bulimia nervosa)*. Eating disorders emerge in the adolescent and early adult years. The high-risk times are puberty and entering secondary school. The patterns of emotions are of anger, rage, loneliness, confusion, withdrawal, fears of separation from parents, problems of control, perfectionism, idealism and dissatisfaction with self. Therefore, protecting our adolescents from the development of eating disorders involves being very positive to them about their appearance; not privileging thinness or commenting on weight; a relaxed approach to food and eating; screening media messages about appearance; protecting them from the possibility of abuse (it is estimated that 90% of women with eating disorders have been sexually abused); not overly-controlling or demanding achievement or perfection and allowing the expression of emotions and of their own identity.

'Identity' is a pivotal issue in adolescence and changes include clothes, hairstyles and the entire appearance of the young person. This is an identity crisis as much for adults as for adolescents. It is not easy to find that one's child has become a blond- or orange-haired specimen overnight; for fathers to see their sons wearing earrings which in their time cast serious doubts on masculinity; for mothers to observe their little girls wearing outfits that are as revealing as a bikini. A delicate balance has to be entered, to guide youngsters and keep them safe from the wrongs and even dangerous interpretation others may make of their appearance, while allowing them some freedom of expression of their independence and attachment to the dictates of the current fashion trends. It hurts to hear, 'You're not going out in that?' Only remarks that are positive are useful.

Indeed, when it comes to teenage stress, the core issue is one of internal identity: Who am I? What am I? What will I become? Identity concerns what teenagers think of themselves, their image of themselves in relation to others, who they are in the present, what they will become in the future. Many of these are worth considering in detail.

How parents react to the identity of the teenager is crucial in reducing the stress for everyone. It can be difficult not to experience their growing up and growing away as rejection, not to grieve for the loss of the little biddable girl or boy. One minute they are parenting a predictable child, made happy with a trip to McDonalds and a Disney video. The next minute they have an unpredictable teenager who would rather be dead than be seen in their company; who scoffs at parental suggestions; takes over the 'phone, the fridge and the house with other rather large and ungainly 'aliens' who go silent when an adult enters the room. But if we try to retain them in the childhood relationship, if we are unable to relinquish control and do not allow the graduated and appropriate taking on of independence, of choice, and of self-control, then both we and the young person suffer great stress in the thwarting of the normal developmental process.

The question, 'Who am I?' is equally confusing for the adolescent in this stage of transition and becoming. 'Am I normal, accepted, attractive, likeable and loveable?', the adolescent wonders. 'Do I fit in? Do I understand myself and do others understand me?' The answer to these questions lies not just with the adolescent and his or her peers, but in the messages we send to them and the answers we give to their questions as parents, educators and as a society. In a survey of young people in Ireland in 1994, in response to the question, 'What influences your life?', 98% identified parents as significant and 65% placed teachers next. Even though adults say that they no longer have any influence over the young, it would seem that this is not the perception of the adolescents themselves. What we say to them and about them is significant in how they define themselves.

In clinical work with adolescents, most will express concern and upset if the relationship with their parents has gone wrong. Most young people love and are loyal to their parents, even if at times they hate the current relationship they may have with each other. Even those who have been suspended from school often wish to return and cope there. The views of teachers are very significant in their evaluation of themselves. It is amazing to watch youngsters who have been regarded as the most 'hardened' speak with pride of a positive remark made by a teacher and ruminate with anger and pain if they felt put down in school. Do we know what power we have as adults to define the young and that they often enact and live out our definitions?

The question of 'What am I?' is therefore an even more difficult question for many adolescents. As a group, they manage to acquire perhaps the greatest range of negative descriptions of any group. They are often regarded as delinquent, unruly, rebellious, hostile, oppositional, disruptive, anti-social, aggressive and selfish. The list of negative attributes is endless and the sad reality is that many adolescents come to believe the messages that are conveyed to them about themselves and to live out these descriptions. Adolescents struggling intellectually or emotionally in school often conceal their difficulties in disruptive behaviour and acquire many of these descriptions and behaviours. Adolescents who are unhappy may be irritable, sullen or angry, particularly if they cannot name their distress. Separating what the person is, from what they pretend to be is an important step in moving from these descriptions and behaviours to the many other positive aspects of the person. Looking beyond the behaviour, to the *meaning or message* is the first step. With whom does this young person show anger, aggression? With whom do they not show these things? What are the situations in which they show negativity, hostility? What are the circumstances in which they might show different emotions? Behaviour that is difficult or aggressive may sometimes be the only way for a person to say, 'I'm in pain, I need attention, I can't cope'.

In answer to the question, 'What will I become?' adolescents often feel that they cannot cope with school and with the future. Even young people who have clearly decided what they would like to do can feel the stress of getting the Junior Certificate or the points in the Leaving Certificate or getting a place in college or on a course or in an apprenticeship or in a job. As adults, we can be there with a strong message of support, providing attention if learning problems arise, and by recognising all talents – not just academic achievement – and supporting the adolescent in making their own choices (not ours) for the future. We can help young people experiencing difficulty at school by calling on teachers, form tutors and school guidance counsellors;

and by seeking educational or psychological assessments. These can help by identifying learning problems and specific learning difficulties such as written language disorders (reading, spelling and writing disorders); specific maths problems or language disorders (difficulty in expressing ideas, in understanding instructions or in relating or communicating with others). Without help, adolescents may become disruptive, anxious, or just give up. Help is available and with renewed self-esteem adolescents can take on the tasks of study, whatever their ability.

Establishing *friendships and social identity* within and outside school is important for adolescents' self-esteem. While most adolescents want to be popular there is also a strong wish for close friends, and intense friendships are more likely to arise in adolescence, particularly amongst girls. One of the important functions of the peer group is to provide a source of information and comparison about the world outside the family. Making and retaining friendships is one of the learning experiences and stresses of adolescence which allows information and evaluation of whether the adolescent is the same as others of their own age – a task which cannot be achieved at home where brothers or sisters are either older or younger. Friendships allow the testing of roles, of gender roles, of being cooperative or competitive amongst equals. Secure family relations are regarded as the basis for entry into the peer system and for success within it, while some studies suggest that with the erosion of the family system, adolescents are thrown into being overly-reliant on peers and are more vulnerable to negative pressure. Although parents may worry about peer pressure, this tends to be less of a negative influence in adolescents who experience themselves as secure and valued within the family.

Friends can be a positive influence if they share positive values and aspirations. Friends can relieve the stress of the adolescent years by being there to share worries and concerns over fear of exams and the future, and as sources of confidences and validation. What is a greater worry is when a young person has not managed to make friends. The adolescent who is isolated or withdrawn, who is bullied or excluded is under enormous stress and this is one of the primary signals that an adolescent is entering deep distress requiring professional intervention.

The search for identity consistent with gender, with being male and female, is a particular stress and very different for boys and girls. One study has demonstrated that male identity is threatened by intimacy and female identity is threatened by separation, which makes understanding each other difficult for adolescents. The portrayal of men and women in the media, and in pornographic magazines and videos, to which adolescents would appear to have virtually unrestricted access, sends a powerful objectifying message of the female body and a powerful macho, aggressive message of coercive sexuality to young men. These may be the means by which adolescents learn about sexuality (in one Irish study of over 1,000 adolescents, 70.9% of first years had seen sexually explicit videos). As adults we can intervene by challenging such messages, by protecting our young people from their influence, and by providing a different interpretation of gender, particularly in the role models we provide.

Adolescent sexuality is too complex to be treated comprehensively in a single chapter but it is certainly bound up with the messages a society conveys about sexuality and sexual behaviour. There is a confusion and proliferation of messages about sexuality, and adolescents in Ireland today would still appear to be largely uneducated in relationships as opposed to anatomical facts. One Irish study has suggested that males hold more promiscuous attitudes than females. Other studies show that there are many derogatory words for active female sexuality but that no derogatory word exists for male sexuality. Specifically, there are 220 words that refer to the sexually promiscuous female and only 20 to the sexually promiscuous male. The language of sexuality continues to be bound up with double standards (female 'slut' vs. male 'stud') which send powerful messages to young people. In this context, the stress of establishing a sexual identity is left with the adolescent. The clinical impression is that this is a considerable stress and struggle for them in a society of mixed messages.

Adolescent suicide is one of the most tragic, sad and unnecessary events, the severing of all the possibilities and potentialities of a young life. It is often a desperate cry for help that is not heard in time. It is the signal of ultimate stress, distress and despair. What happens when the normal stresses of adolescence escalate to the levels of distress that would lead a young person to end their life? What happens when the spots, the greasy hair, poor body-image, poor self-esteem, the problems with friends, struggles at school, bullying, isolation, lack of love, loneliness and conflict, without a sense of support from adults or friends, accumulate into a picture of real despair? Again, this is too complex a subject to analyse fully here but the following are guidelines for the identification of depression and feelings of despair in adolescents.

One important measure in keeping adolescents safe is not to dismiss what may be their real pain to the category of adolescent moods or irritability, and treat them as 'just a phase'. Signs of depression include: the young person loses interest in activities; does not respond or even feel better when something good happens; is more upset in the morning; is sleeping badly or waking up early; is losing weight, complains of being tired or shows loss of energy; expresses feelings of worthlessness or guilt, and becomes tearful, sad and withdrawn. Suicide and attempted suicide are practically unknown in children but begin to appear at puberty and increase throughout adolescence and can reach a peak in late teens. Troubles with parents, friends or school are the most prominent signs and if there are difficulties for them in all these contexts we need to be particularly vigilant. Adolescents often feel lonely, unwanted or angry. Sometimes, acts of self-poisoning are attempts to alleviate these feelings or draw attention to them that go wrong and end tragically. Threats of suicide should always be taken seriously. They are cries for help. Adolescents' feelings need to be heard. In the radio series accompanying this book, a boy called David gave a poignant example of how adolescent stresses mounted into a wish to kill himself. He equally showed that when given an opportunity to be heard, to understand his feelings and the actions of others, to understand his parents who really did care and to take a break from pressure, that he could progress to good functioning towards adulthood.

Family breakup and the sense of loss experienced by youngsters when parents separate, divorce and particularly when they form new relationships that involve having further children, can be a source of enormous stress. Feelings of rejection, guilt, anger and fear are caused. Initially, at least, adolescents need to spend time alone with the parent who has left as opposed to time shared with their new partner. They must not be expected to welcome the arrival of a new baby into the new relationship or relationships. They need time to grieve for the loss of the family as they knew it and to have their grief validated. Adolescent boys need their fathers as role models and, while men have often felt excluded from parenting, their importance cannot be overestimated. Adolescent girls also need the continuing warmth and care of their fathers if they are to enter into trustful relationships later with men. Mothers need support if continuing the primary care of children. New relationships by mothers may make youngsters anxious and angry, and both these emotions need to be recognised and validated. Despite the longitudinal studies of children of separation, we have yet to see in this country the social and clinical impact of separation. So far, the clinical findings are alerting us to the severe disruption caused to the adolescent process, the degree of misery and confusion that arises for young people and the need for very careful and attentive handling and support for young people.

Everything to be said about helping adolescents depends on our *relationship* with them. Indeed, relationship is central to adolescent/ parent interactions and the following examines some of the relationship issues relevant to the growing up process.

Ideally, helping adolescents through the stress of adolescence begins long before adolescence in a relationship which is warm, caring and respectful and one in which clear boundaries of behaviour have been established in a gentle but firm way. The child who is praised, encouraged, told they are wonderful, look great, who has always felt valued, will be more able to listen to a parent's views or concern about them later. They will be more able to attend to rules if the pre-adolescent rules have appeared to be fair and reasonable and consistent. Consistency (not rigidity) in rules carries into the adolescent years.

While adolescents do seek more time alone and away from their parents, they also want parents to be available when they need them and to feel that the parent is still there for them. Sometimes, we need to seek them out, knock on the bedroom door, ask about their day, their worries, their interests. We may get monosyllabic responses like 'fine', 'okay', 'nothing', but the asking is appreciated even if not shown. Many adolescents are hurt when their ideas are dismissed. Listening is crucial to maintaining a relationship. We listen attentively to the often garbled stories of children and we do not usually correct or object to the ideas in these stories, although we might suggest another way of thinking or acting or ending the story. Adolescence is no different. What has been called the 'arrogance of youth' is often the adolescent's first strident statements about how things are or should be and are to be admired, not ridiculed. A parent can often help with the stress of new ideas by acknowledging that there are injustices in the world, by asking how they would deal with them differently, and by commending them for caring. Being listened to is high on the list of priorities for adolescents in relating to the adult world and in reducing their stress.

Although concerns about *drug abuse* are associated most with adolescents, statistics show that the greater abusers of drugs (once we include legalised drugs such as cigarettes and alcohol) are adults. To combat the concerted efforts of drug pushers it is essential to be informed about drugs, to know where adolescents are at all times and who they are with, and to be vigilant for any signs of abuse by them. The primary signs that an adolescent might be using drugs are: sudden mood swings, loss of interest in previously enjoyed activities, great and uncharacteristic irritability or aggression, change in school performance, change of 'friends' whose visits or phonecalls seem to make the adolescent fearful, money or objects disappearing from the home, lying or furtive behaviour, sleepiness, poor appetite, and sores or spots on arms, mouth or nose.

Just as with the toddler during a temper tantrum, when we hold or contain their frustration and do not participate in their anger, so too do we need to contain the adolescent during the clash of wills and the stresses and frustrations they experience. Usually, we are not angry with the young child who can't contain frustration. In many ways the adolescent is no different, except that their larger physical size makes the tantrum all the more alarming and makes us more likely to respond with anger or with physical control. Sometimes, they are out of control and we may also feel that we have lost all control. We have not if we listen, allow the anger to be expressed and abate and quietly hold firm to a reasonable rule.

Perhaps one of the most dangerous and hurtful statements we can make to an adolescent is, 'If you don't like it you can leave'. Those who require clinical attention have often found themselves in a cycle of clashes with parents that has ended with this statement. Parents rarely mean it, but adolescents can respond by running away, by testing parents to the limit to see if they would really throw them out, or by losing all trust in their parents' love for them. When things go drastically wrong it is helpful to say, 'We can get through this together', to let them know you still love them and that you will seek professional help for everyone.

Allied to the above, one of the most important messages to adolescents is that we will always stand by them, will never give up on them and that they will always be our daughter or son. This is not to collude in serious acts like covering up mistakes the adolescent makes. Adolescents who know that their parents will stand by them, while also making them take responsibility for their actions, are at much less risk of rash acts and if they do occur they can be valuable learning experiences, not the end of the relationship.

Part of growing up at any stage of life, is being allowed to safely make mistakes. We let the child ride a bike even if they occasionally fall off. Adolescents also need safe opportunities to learn and to make mistakes. What they appreciate most is the way their parents talk about it when mistakes are made rather than responding with uncontrollable anger and punishment. As an example, if the young person comes home much later than agreed the parents might say that they realise that they made a mistake in allowing them to go without collecting them. The task of adolescence is to move away from parental authority to authority over themselves and therefore it is bound to be a time of errors and mistakes by all of us.

Despite ideas to the contrary, young people really appreciate firm and clear boundaries and rules about behaviour. Most adolescents will admit that they like to have rules. If the rule is for coming home at 11.00 p.m. then they feel safe in pushing to come home at 11.15 p.m. or 11.30 p.m. Having rules is a sign of caring and is a powerful message of love.

When we know where our young people are, we are not being intrusive. We are being caring, particularly in a world where there are so many dangers for young people especially in the younger stages of adolescence when they are most at risk. Starting when they are young and giving the message that safety is the primary concern makes it easier to find a workable passage through the process. Implementing rules firmly but with fairness and understanding can dilute or help avoid clashes.

I hesitate to make a list of what to do or not to do, because all of us who are parenting adolescents or who work with them find our own way towards a better understanding of them and of their needs.

However, I would suggest that the following may be helpful in our relationship with young people:

- Listen to the messages behind the words and behaviour.
- Be available, not intrusive.
- Be in control, not controlling.
- Be clear, be comfortable, be confident, you know the young person better than anyone.
- Don't try to reason too much, a good rule and a safe rule doesn't need changing.
- Don't be afraid to say 'no' appropriately, particularly where issues of safety are involved.
- Make safety the primary issue and the guide to what you will allow.
- Know at all times where they are, who they are with – you have the right to keep them safe.
- Don't be afraid to act like a parent. Don't try to look or act like a teenager. Adolescents still need guidance and will respect this as they move into adulthood.
- Don't say 'you are not going there because you will get into trouble', but rather 'I cannot let you go there because I am worried about your safety'.
- Avoid conflicts about appearance, clothes, hairstyles, make-up, untidy bedrooms – they are not life-threatening.
- Be encouraging, praising, supportive, gentle, loving. We all thrive on these.
- Find opportunities to compliment their talents, their ideas, their appearance, their behaviour.
- Avoid criticism as adolescent self-esteem is fragile. If necessary, criticise the behaviour, not the person.
- Be careful not to joke or ridicule your teenager, or young people in general.
- Don't embarrass them in front of friends, deal with the issue when they are alone.
- Remember, you cannot buy a teenager's love or affection. However, be generous if you can, so they have enough of the things their friends have (e.g. fashion).
- Explain and sympathise if you can't afford a reasonable request. They may complain but they will understand.

- Screen the messages that come to them through the media and challenge the negative ones.
- Know and spot signs of increased stress, distress and depression and act immediately.
- Know the signs if they are being bullied and deal with the problem immediately. Let them know they have your support, sympathy and action.
- Be vigilant for signs of substance abuse and take charge.
- Give the teenager space to grow.
- Trust your instincts and abilities – you love them more than anyone else.
- Come to terms with the fact that your child must grow up. Don't grieve for the child, look forward to the adult.

Today's adolescents are emotionally no different than at any other time. For them, life is intense, emotional, dramatic, funny and tragic and there is still the child within them wanting to be protected. But most of all there is the person who, like everyone else, wants to be loved, respected, accepted and to get it right. How they and we cope with the normal and even abnormal stresses of this time depends on our relationship.

Ultimately, we must let them go and how successfully we do so depends on the quality of the relationship we have established throughout the teenage years. Remember, however, that adolescence is a natural process. At the end of the day, it is the process of growing up. It is not an illness and time is the only cure.

Panic

by

Myra Doherty

Each of us has experienced anxiety and panic to some degree in our lives, especially at times of danger or threat to our safety or to the safety of loved ones. This is a normal bodily response that enables us to take the immediate action that is necessary for survival and is often referred to as *fight or flight*. After the danger has passed these feelings subside and we feel safe again. We should be thankful for the ability of our body and mind to instantly and automatically respond in such instances. However, at times, this emergency system can go astray.

A *Panic Attack* is a terrifying experience during which the body responds with many of the same physiological changes that take place during an emergency. These physiological changes include an increased heart rate, palpitations, dizziness, nausea and feelings of unreality. The difference is that this arousal due to panic occurs in the absence of any real danger or threat. These bodily reactions, necessary in times of danger, are normal and not harmful. When they occur in a panic attack the symptoms, while harmless, are remembered by those who have had a panic attack as one of the most uncomfortable states a human being is capable of experiencing. The physical sensations of fear escalate with amazing speed until it feels as if something catastrophic might happen, like collapsing, losing control, having a heart attack or dying. The panic usually peaks within the first few minutes, and the sensations then subside, but more slowly than they started.

It is not surprising, given how terrifying panic attacks can be, that once experienced, confidence can be greatly shaken. Some people live in dread of further attacks, searching for ways of ensuring that they will not happen again. Panic attacks are difficult to understand and come to terms with and their effects may persist, partly because it is hard to understand what precipitated them. Even people who can recognise the situations that make them susceptible to panic, such as crowded areas, queues, or speaking in public, are often at a loss to explain exactly what triggered a particular attack. They believe it came on 'out of the blue', and they live in fear of the next one.

Typically the onset of the disorder begins in early adulthood, with a female to male prevalence ratio of almost 2:1. The reasons for the high presentation in females is unclear, but many men who present for treatment describe how difficult it is to seek help for their problems, due to embarrassment and fear of being laughed at. Others describe how they use alcohol to alleviate their symptoms.

There is no single agreed cause for the disorder. However, it is accepted that stress, anxiety and significant life events are associated with the onset of panic attacks. Some studies suggest that the prevalence of life events in the years preceding the onset of panic attacks is greater than for those who don't have this problem.

Given the intensity of the symptoms it is not unusual or surprising that many people go to their local Accident and Emergency Department for immediate treatment and help. One lady in therapy recalled how she developed a pattern for staying safe. This included driving with her husband to his work in the morning and, after dropping him off, spending the remainder of the day parked in the local hospital grounds.

She told me she felt safe knowing that medical help was available close by, when she had what she perceived to be the heart attack. Another woman recalled how she spent a large amount of time when alone in her home, on the telephone talking to various friends, in the belief that they would be able to quickly summon medical help if she needed it, and despite running up a large telephone bill she continued to use this as a coping method. Both of these women had undergone investigations, including electrocardiographs. They were told by their doctors that all tests were normal. Initially, both women found it very difficult to relate these frightening symptoms to anxiety and panic as it is hard to believe that such a dramatic event could happen without there being something seriously wrong.

The prevalence of panic attacks and panic disorder in medical settings is high, and more people suffering panic attacks are seen in medical settings than in psychiatric settings. This is understandable given the nature of panic attacks. Their sudden and unexpected arrival leaves the victim wondering when the next attack will strike. Since the symptoms may start without a clear-cut precipitant it is reasonable that many at first interpret them as a manifestation of a medical illness. Typically, sufferers may select one symptom from their experience and seek out specialists to investigate that problem. For example, as in the two cases described earlier, a cardiologist may be consulted for palpitations or chest pains. In other cases they may seek referral to a neurologist for headaches, dizziness or light-headedness.

THE MAIN SYMPTOMS OF PANIC ARE:

Physical Sensations
- *Light-headedness*
- *Dizziness*
- *Vertigo*
- *Faintness*
- *Tremors*
- *Numbness, prickly feeling in the arms and face*
- *Sweating*
- *Chest pain, palpitations or accelerated heart rate*
- *Nausea or vomiting*
- *Choking sensation; dry mouth, breathlessness*
- *Depersonalisation or feelings of unreality*

Behavioural patterns
- *Leaving the situations*
- *Gripping furniture for support, e.g. chair, trolley*
- *Sitting down, or going to bed*

Emotions
- *Fear*
- *Terror/panic*

Thoughts
- *Something awful is happening to me*
- *I am going mad/losing control*
- *I am having a heart attack*
- *I am dying*

For most people the panic attacks experienced may precipitate the onset of *Phobias* or *Avoidance Behaviour* over the following months. The circumstances in which the original panic attack occurred and the intensity of the attacks experienced, associated with the initial location, usually determine the particular phobia that follows. A phobia can be defined as a fear of a situation that is out of proportion to its danger, can neither be explained nor reasoned away, is largely beyond voluntary control and leads to avoidance of a feared situation. If a person experiences a panic attack in the church or in a supermarket, that event by association becomes capable of triggering high levels of anticipatory anxiety in the future. The anticipatory anxiety can often precipitate the very thing feared. In other words, if you are expecting to panic, the expectation works like a self-fulfilling prophecy. The next time that person thinks about going shopping or to the church, or indeed attempts to go, they may recall the previously experienced anxiety. The individual may decide to avoid going in order to remain safe, or enter the feared situation and leave within minutes.

If this avoidance persists, and as frequently occurs, leads to further avoidance, the term agoraphobia with panic attacks is used. Over time, multiple avoidant behaviour develops. *Agoraphobia* is a very common condition. It is estimated that approximately 60–80% of all phobics are agoraphobic. An essential feature is the marked fear of being alone or in public places, from which escape might be difficult, or where help might not be easily available in case of the feared catastrophe.

Very quickly these avoidances can become a disabling complication for people who have suffered panic attacks over a period of time. They lose the confidence to carry on life in a normal way and families are also affected. Very soon they may find they cannot leave the safety of their own home. Research has shown that people who suffer from panic or agoraphobia may become disabled by their symptoms as early as fifteen months after the initial panic attack.

Men and women who present for therapy generally have a number of common questions to ask:

Q. Can a panic attack cause heart failure?

A. Rapid heartbeat and palpitations during a panic attack can be very frightening sensations, but they are rarely dangerous.

Your heart is made up of very strong and dense muscle fibres and can withstand a lot more than you think. During a true heart attack the most common symptom is continuous pain and a feeling of pressure or a crushing sensation in the centre of your chest. Moreover, the pain and pressure get worse with exertion and may tend to diminish with rest. This is quite different from a panic attack, where racing and pounding may get worse if you stand still and lessen if you move around.

Q. Can a panic attack cause suffocation or cessation of breathing?

A. It is common during a panic attack for your breathing to feel restricted. Under stress, your neck and chest muscles are tightening and reducing your respiratory capacity. Your brain has a built-in reflex mechanism that will eventually force you to breathe if you're not getting enough oxygen. So, no matter how distressing choking and sensations of constriction are during panic, they are not dangerous.

Q. Can a panic attack cause me to faint?

A. When light-headedness is experienced during a panic attack it may evoke a fear of fainting. It is not unusual for people who suffer from panic attacks to breathe about twice as fast as normal, which may lead to dizziness, and eventually this shorter, rapid breathing may lead to hyperventilation. This is not dangerous and can be relieved quickly by breathing slowly and regularly from the abdomen, preferably through the nose. Hyperventilation occurs any time a person breathes in such a way that they breathe out more carbon dioxide than their body is manufacturing.

Q. Can a panic attack cause insanity?

A. No one has ever gone crazy from a panic attack, even though the fear of doing so is very common. As bad as they feel, these sensations of unreality will eventually pass and are completely harmless.

Q. Can a panic attack cause loss of control?

A. Because of the intense physical changes experienced during panic, it is easy to imagine that you could 'completely lose it'. For some, this may mean acting uncontrollably, or a fear that they may run screaming from the scene. This does not happen.

The only thing that happens is that people quickly leave the scene of the panic and this is not loss of control. This occurs because of the body's natural in-built survival mechanism, which causes the *fight or flight* response in situations that generally threaten your survival.

Q. Is taking alcohol to relieve the symptoms of anxiety harmful?

A. Yes, using alcohol in order to cope with anxiety is dangerous. You may become physically or psychologically dependent. The danger with physical dependence is that if you stop drinking you may experience withdrawal symptoms such as acute anxiety and restlessness. This withdrawal may be dangerous and it can be potentially life-threatening. If you have been using alcohol heavily, in order to cope, discuss the problem with your General Practitioner as it can be dangerous to cease drinking without medical supervision. With psychological dependence, alcohol comes to feel as if it is essential. Your ability to lead a normal daily life becomes more restricted and gradually you lose confidence. Alcohol can boost confidence in the short-term, but does not help recovery in the long-term.

Q. How long will therapy last?

A. Cognitive Behavioural Therapy is relatively short-term and generally involves 5–10 sessions. The responsibility for recovery rests largely with the client in so far as the amount of work you do in the form of homework between sessions can help to determine the rate of recovery. Initially, this is difficult as you are learning to face previously avoided situations and activities, but with prolonged, gradual exposure and positive coping techniques your anxiety will level off and decrease to an acceptable level. (The use of positive coping techniques is explained at a later stage in the chapter). It does not matter how slowly you progress, as long as you are practising you will continue to make progress and will get there in the end.

Before undergoing any treatment for panic disorder it is important to undergo a thorough medical examination to rule out other possible causes of the distressing symptoms. This is necessary because a number of other conditions, such as excessive levels of thyroid hormone, certain types of epilepsy or cardiac arrhythmias (which are disturbances in the rhythm of the heartbeat) can cause symptoms resembling those of panic disorder.

We live in a fortunate time for those who suffer from anxiety, panic attacks and agoraphobia. The decade of the 1980s saw advances in research and treatment in two major areas:

The first was in the development of minor tranquillisers, which are powerful enough to ward off panic attacks, but do not cure them. They become less effective over time and may be addictive. In addition to the use of minor tranquillisers, anti-depressant medication has also been agreed to be effective in the treatment of panic attacks. It is not addictive, but the symptoms of panic tend to return when the medication is stopped. The problems of reoccurrence of symptoms on withdrawal of medication, as well as issues relating to resistance to medication and intolerance of side-effects, are common. Withdrawal symptoms from minor tranquillisers are unpleasant and vary from person to person. Many of the more common ones are similar to the symptoms of anxiety. They can include sweating, shaking, disturbed sleep, poor concentration and a sensation of your heart speeding up. Therefore, medicines can be both a help and a hindrance to overcoming panic attacks. For some sufferers medication is essential, especially when psychological methods have proved unsuccessful or are unacceptable. A medical doctor should always monitor a person's medication. It is very important not to stop taking medication unless under the strict supervision of your medical doctor.

The second major development in the treatment of panic attacks was the development of cognitive behavioural therapy. This is a combination of cognitive therapy which can help identify unhelpful thought patterns which may contribute to the individual's symptoms, and exposure therapy which aims to reduce avoidant behaviour and help the individual face the anxiety-provoking situations regularly and repeatedly, in a graded way, until anxiety diminishes to an acceptable level.

During initial assessment, the therapist may use a number of self-rating questionnaires, in order to help determine the severity of the problem, prior to the commencement of treatment. These may be beneficial especially if you have been suffering from panic attacks for a number of years. The questionnaires help measure general levels of fear and anxiety, and help identify overt and covert avoidances that may serve to maintain the problem.

The cognitive model states that individuals with panic disorder often have distortion in their thinking. For example, they may complain of their heart beating fast, tightness in the chest, or nausea. This sensation may have been triggered by some worry, an unpleasant mental image, minor illness, or even physical exercise. The person with panic disorder responds to these sensations by becoming anxious. This anxiety triggers still more unpleasant sensations which in turn heighten anxiety, giving rise to catastrophic thoughts. For example: 'I'm having a heart attack', or 'I'm going insane'. As the vicious circle continues a panic attack results.

If you feel you are suffering from panic disorder and have not yet sought treatment, I would encourage you to discuss your symptoms with your General Practitioner. In consultation with him/her, you may decide that a self-help group or a self-help guide may be sufficient, that is if your problem is not too disabling. It may also be helpful before beginning a self-help approach to enlist the support of a family member or trusted friend as co-therapist. They can help, support and encourage you throughout treatment, especially on the bad days, when you feel you are not making any progress. It is important to remember that setbacks are part of recovery and what seemed relatively easy to accomplish yesterday, may seem impossible today. Your confidence is bound to fluctuate, so apparent setbacks are a normal part of progress. They are disappointing, but not a sign of failure. There are a number of techniques which may be helpful when beginning a self-help programme, and these are now outlined briefly.

Coping with anticipatory anxiety

As mentioned earlier, anticipatory anxiety can often precipitate the very thing feared. Therefore, it is important to learn to deal with it. If you begin to feel anxious, recognise consciously that this is anxiety caused by the misinterpretation of something harmless. Remind yourself that the feelings of anxiety are not due to physical illness and are not signs of insanity. The body has no way of knowing if a stressful situation is real or imagined unless the brain tells it, so it is very important to learn to recognise those negative, fear-producing thoughts that have the power to turn a safe environment into a place of anxiety and panic.

Overcoming avoidance

The desire to avoid situations associated with anxiety and panic is natural, but in the long-term may make the problem worse. You lose self-confidence and things that were once easy to do become difficult; for example, going to shops or social gatherings and using public transport. If you continually avoid these situations you fail to learn that nothing bad will happen and that the sensations are harmless. The fear spreads quickly to other situations and you gradually avoid them more and more. Try to identify all the situations and activities that you avoid and arrange them in order of difficulty. Begin with the easiest task on your list and practice this until your anxiety decreases to an acceptable level. Gradually move through the list of avoided situations and activities until you reach the most difficult. Expect to feel anxious and remember that panic is caused by a sudden surge of adrenalin, a chemical that is released into the body in preparation for danger. However, there is no real danger, only the perception of danger. Stay in the situation until your anxiety decreases to an acceptable level. Use positive coping statements such as, 'This is anxiety, it's unpleasant but it is not dangerous'. View each episode as an opportunity to practice new coping skills and to learn more about the sort of things that trigger your panic. By understanding that the panic attack is not dangerous, the fear of the panic attack itself diminishes. People who suffer from panic attacks tend to overestimate the risks they face and to underestimate their ability to cope. By learning to recognise, and then to change these distorted ways of thinking, you will overcome your fear.

Breathing Retraining

Proper breathing control may be necessary to control over-breathing or hyperventilation. Practice breathing slowly, in through your nose and out through your mouth. You should practice this many times when you are not anxious, before using it to control the symptoms of panic.

Relaxation Techniques

Relaxation is one of the most general ways of making you feel better. For many people, the ability to relax is not something that comes easily, but must be learned. By practising relaxation regularly you may acquire more energy and decrease levels of tension and anxiety. There are many aids to help you relax, such as muscular relaxation tapes. Ask your General Practitioner to recommend a suitable method for you.

Distraction Techniques

It is important to avoid self-monitoring and hypervigilance of symptoms as this will only make them worse. The more you focus on the internal symptoms, such as palpitations, dizziness, etc. the more you will feel that there is something wrong with your body, and the more likely you will be to misinterpret them and trigger another panic attack. The use of distraction techniques can be very beneficial. Instead of focusing on what is happening to you, try to focus on events around you. This could involve mental exercises such as arithmetic or doing a crossword puzzle or physical activity such as going for a walk or simply keeping busy. The following example may help illustrate this technique: 'I'm sitting in a room, with four other people. The walls are painted cream and the carpet is brown. One of the others, a man, is wearing a black coat with a white shirt', etc.

Panic attacks are very frightening for sufferers and affect all aspects of their daily life. If untreated the individual can become restricted. It is relatively easy to treat with patience, understanding and education. If you are suffering in silence, hoping the problem will go away, then take heart and consult your General Practitioner as soon as possible, because help is available. Research has shown that cognitive behavioural therapy is an effective treatment for panic attacks, and studies suggest that the success rates are as high as 80–90%. If, following a consultation with your General Practitioner, you feel a self-help programme is of little benefit, then they may decide to refer you to a therapist in your local area.

5

Food and Stress

by

Dr John Griffin

Stress is part of everyday life – we all experience stress, at one time or another. From the psychological viewpoint, the most important aspect is how we react to that stress. Much has been written in the lay and medical literature in recent decades about this subject. Numerous articles and books have been published, many radio and television documentaries have been aired, even the agony aunts have been asked to respond countless times to questions about stress. Stress is inevitable in our modern 'fast track world'. We can react to this by various coping mechanisms described in other chapters in this book or we can suffer from the effects of stress. This suffering may be apparent in a purely physical way, e.g. raised blood pressure, a purely psychological response – best described as 'feeling under pressure' or most commonly in a psychosomatic way. This latter refers to both physical and psychological symptoms being present at the same time and these symptoms being interdependent, i.e. usually what begins as 'feeling under pressure' produces physical symptoms like a rapid heartbeat, sweaty palms, butterflies in the stomach, even moderate to severe chest pain. These physical manifestations of stress, especially the latter one, serve only to heighten the terror that the sufferer experiences. Often, at this stage, the person will imagine they are going to get a heart attack or a stroke. People can go on with these symptoms for years before coming for proper medical help. To summarise then, stress is inevitable in our daily lives – it's how we cope with stress that matters.

How then can we relate food and stress? There has been considerable discussion and debate in recent years about the increase in eating disorders in the western world. Over the past 30 years a rather dramatic change has occurred in socio-cultural perceptions of body weight and body image. The condemnation of obesity as being ugly and undesirable in the western world and the constant cultural pressure toward slimness are facts of modern day living. The social stigma against obesity is extraordinary in its magnitude and pervasiveness. Public derision and condemnation of fat people is one of the few remaining social prejudices. The affront to those who are obese goes beyond the almost uniform judgement that they are unattractive and includes negative stereotypes that begin in early childhood. Think, for example, of the words that people associate with obesity or fatness – words such as 'laziness', 'ugliness' and 'stupidity' come to mind. Contrast this with the words that might nowadays be associated with slimness – words such as attractive, healthy, even sexy, come to mind.

What has changed society's outlook on body weight and image in the past three decades? To answer this, it is necessary to look back to the earlier decades of this century. Let's start with the 1929 Wall Street Crash. This was followed by a severe depression, particularly in the United States. On the first of September 1939, Adolf Hitler invaded Poland and two days later Britain declared war on Germany. Thus, the Second World War came into being (I appreciate, for historical purists, that there were many other factors involved also). Food was scarce in Europe during the period 1939 to 1945 and indeed rationing continued for many years after the Second World War. It is interesting to note that the first major scientific papers describing *Anorexia Nervosa* were not published until the 1950s and most of those papers emanated from the United States. Hilde Bruch's classical treatise on Anorexia Nervosa is a good example. The United States was not a theatre of war and thus recovered much more quickly following the ending of hostilities. Thus, relative affluence and plenty came to the United States rather sooner than to mainland Europe or to these islands. This point is relevant because modern eating disorders are described only in western countries and not in countries where starvation is a daily fact of life. I have yet to read of a study of these eating disorders emanating from Third World countries where a bowl of rice a day is often the staple diet

Anorexia Nervosa is best described as 'the relentless pursuit of excessive thinness'. What drives young teenage girls (95% of cases are female) to lose a huge amount of weight, exercise obsessively, self-induce vomiting, abuse laxatives and at all costs avoid food due to morbid fear of fatness? To answer this in part, I need to refer to the desirable female figure of the 1940s and 1950s. For example, most people would be surprised to learn that Marilyn Monroe took a size 16. However, in the mid-60s a particular model, named Twiggy, walked down the catwalk and stunned the fashion world by being so different. This model was very slim and since then fashion houses appear to favour young slim models. It is generally accepted that the socio-cultural model offers the most supported theoretical explanation for our society's high level of body image disturbance, body dissatisfaction and the increasing rate of eating disorders among women. By presenting women with 'a constant barrage of idealised images of extremely thin women', the media promote standards that are impossible for most women to achieve. The resulting pursuit of thinness has important consequences in terms of lowered self-esteem, excessive dieting practices and the emergence of serious eating disorders.

Television is arguably the most prominent and influential form of the mass media, especially for adolescents. Not only do young people watch the most television, but it has been suggested that the societal pressures of thinness are particularly influential during adolescence and young adulthood. This is, of course, the time for gender identity development and sex role exploration. A recent study noted it was *what* girls watched that matters. In particular, time reported watching soaps, serials and movies – programmes likely to show women in stereotyped roles – positively correlated with body dissatisfaction. Music videos were particularly 'damaging', especially in relation to this drive for thinness. Maybe this is because music videos provide the opportunity for explicit comparison with others. Thus, I would suggest that one of the most common stresses that females have to cope with today is this above mentioned 'drive for thinness'. Like all forms of stress, it is a matter of how each individual copes with these pressures that will determine whether or not she suffers in a mild or fleeting way or goes on to develop a full-blown eating disorder.

Let us now look in a little more depth at Anorexia Nervosa. Most women have their first episodes of anorexia in their teens and women who never develop anorexia often feel uncomfortable, especially during their teens, with their newly acquired body shape, wish they were thinner and diet intermittently. Very few people find adolescence and its tasks of forging an adult personality easy. It is a time of many challenges and stresses. At puberty a girl's body begins to change shape and secondary sexual characteristics appear, e.g. the development of pubic hair and breast development. Periods begin and this can be a very anxious and threatening time for the pubertal female.

There are many psychoanalytical theories and models used to explain anorexia, but I will not go into detail about these in this chapter. However, once established, full-blown Anorexia Nervosa can be very difficult to treat. It's almost like a parasite or, as I sometimes describe it, a demonic possession. Parents are often driven to distraction trying to persuade the unwilling young teenager to eat. There are constant rows between the patient and her parents but especially between daughter and mother. The stresses in the home often lead to serious marital disharmony. These anorectic teenagers are excellent at manipulating their parents. They often play off one against the other. The parents may decide on a strategy of 'good cop/bad cop' i.e. one being easy and reassuring with the patient while the other takes a much firmer line. However, the anorectic will very quickly recognise this and use it to her own advantage, causing stress in the parental relationship. I have often suggested that siblings are the forgotten ones in a family with Anorexia Nervosa. Obviously, because the anorectic is getting lots of attention due to the constant battles in the kitchen, the other siblings are often forgotten or at least sidelined to some degree. This can lead to the oft-described problem of sibling rivalry. That's why it is so important in treatment not just to involve the parents but also the siblings as well. Remember this is a family condition, not just an individual one. As any parent who has had to deal with anorexia in the home will tell you, it is an extremely difficult and demanding condition to deal with. They will cite the rows, the tantrums, the screaming matches, the banging of doors, the tears, etc. as examples of the stresses that go on in these families. Sadly, this striving for thinness in full-blown Anorexia Nervosa will continue unless a therapeutic regime is established.

I always suggest that the first consultation with the anorectic and her family is the most important one. I say this for two reasons. First, this may be the only time you will see this child and her family as she may adamantly refuse ever to return if the consultation is badly handled. Second, it is essential at first interview to reassure the patient that you are not going to make her fat and reassure her even further that you will accept 95% of ideal body weight as being reasonable. Before coming into any therapeutic programme, in my opinion it is essential to have at least some degree of commitment and motivation from the patient. Thus, for example, certification or committal to hospital for a treatment programme is generally not effective. The only exception would be when life-saving measures are essential. However, fortunately this is extremely rare in western medicine. Once the patient comes into care, there is a collective sigh of relief from all concerned but especially parents and siblings. Along the way the family are constantly involved in treatment as not just the patient but the family needs to be healed also. Follow-up is absolutely crucial and Professor Arthur Crisp in London, one of the most eminent contributors to this subject, suggests that one can never deem the condition to be fully recovered until five years follow-up has been completed.

Bulimia Nervosa, on the other hand, is a condition of older females, the average age range being 18–25. Thus often girls will have left home and be in college or working independently from their families. The average time a patient has bulimia before coming for medical help is five to six years. This is often because the person feels great shame and disgust at what they are doing, i.e. bingeing and purging, the feeling that they are hopeless cases and nothing can be done for them. Bulimia Nervosa often begins following the break-up of a relationship or some other emotional disturbance in a girl's life. It, like Anorexia Nervosa, is a predominantly female condition. The fact that the sufferer has often left home and is living separately from the family allows the sufferer to continue in secret for many years before she seeks medical help. It begins as a method of dieting but it is often described as a chaotic method of dieting. The patient starves themselves initially and then binges on large amounts of carbohydrate-like food and afterwards either self-induces vomiting or uses large amounts of laxatives to get rid of the food. Thus, the person begins the binge/vomit cycle. Often, patients with this condition describe it almost like an addiction, i.e. a habit that is very difficult to break without medical intervention. Unlike classical Anorexia Nervosa, the vast majority of bulimics can be treated on an out-patient basis.

In the acute stages of the condition, the bulimic is leading an utterly miserable life of secret starving, bingeing and purging. They usually manage to hold down their jobs or a third-level course but the rest of their lives are effectively a mess. For example, they can't eat out socially because they know if they do, they must immediately vomit or purge afterwards. Binges almost always occur in secret. Keeping this secret can involve considerable subterfuge and deception. Typically, the food eaten in a binge is consumed very quickly. It is almost wolfed down. Initially, the sufferer may have a sense of pleasure but this disappears very quickly. Patients with Bulimia Nervosa describe a powerful craving for food and a feeling that they are being driven to eat huge amounts. The desperation people feel drives them to behave in ways quite alien to their character. Following self-induced vomiting there is an initial sense of relief, followed by feelings of shame, guilt and disgust. Depression is common after binges and purging as people feel hopeless about ever being able to control their eating. Out-patient treatment programmes consist of the selection of a co-therapist, e.g. a best friend, spouse, partner or somebody in whom the person feels comfortable in confiding. The initial consultation is held alone with the patient and all further consultations are held with the consultant, patient and 'co-therapist'. The person is asked to keep a diary of all foods they consume and also to note each time they have vomited or abused laxatives. They are also asked to write down any urges to binge, vomit or abuse laxatives. They are asked to discuss this diary with their co-therapist each day and to bring it along to the regular consultations with their consultant. The only weighing allowed is once weekly which must be in the company of a co-therapist and this must be done on the same scales, at the same time of day, wearing the same clothes, to exclude as many variables as possible.

The concepts of availability and opportunity must be discussed. Availability refers to the easy access to binge foods, e.g. high calorie, high carbohydrate foods, and opportunity refers obviously to the ease with which the patient can indulge in binges. Patients are asked to keep all of the 'binge foods' away from their larders and not to have enough money easily available to them each day to purchase these foods. Thus, it becomes increasingly more difficult for the bulimic to have access to the types of food she will most likely binge on. From the opportunity point of view it is best that the bulimic eats in company at all times and tries to have her evening meal with her co-therapist. Most bulimics tend to do their bingeing and vomiting in the evening and can usually manage a small breakfast or snack at lunchtime without purging. Following the ingestion of their evening meal with their co-therapist, they are not allowed to visit the toilet for at least an hour after the ingestion of their food so that self-induced vomiting is much less likely. This is a very basic description of the behaviour programme that is used for Bulimia Nervosa. Obviously, family therapy is also essential in this condition if the sufferer is still living with her family, or if the family has become involved in the treatment programme.

Binge-eating disorder has only been described in the past four years. This is a condition similar to Bulimia Nervosa but without the compensatory self-induced vomiting or purging. This is a rather similar condition to compulsive overeating. Multi-impulsive bulimia has also been recently described by Hubert Lacey, who is attached to St George's Hospital in London. This is a condition where the bulimic displays other behaviour such as cutting, shoplifting, abusing alcohol, taking street drugs or overdosing. The stress caused by all of these conditions is obviously enormous while the patient remains untreated.

Like every other condition in medicine, prevention is the best cure, but if this is not possible, early intervention is obviously most desirable. Every study has shown that the earlier eating disorder patients come to help the better the prognosis. For the past decade or so I have been asked to speak to various secondary schools around the country about the dangers of eating disorders. However, I am usually asked by headmasters and headmistresses to speak to fifth and sixth year classes. I wonder whether speaking to this population is leaving it a little too late, and whether or not one should be concentrating on girls in their last year in primary school. As described above, puberty is the commonest time for the onset of Anorexia Nervosa and perhaps a programme of education about the dangers of eating disorders would be more suited either in sixth year in primary school or at the latest in first or second year in secondary school. Also, perhaps a medical consultant is not the best person to speak to this population. Perhaps a recovering anorectic or bulimic might be a person much more suited to this task.

In recent years an excellent organisation called 'BODYWHYS' has been established in Ireland. This is a self-help organisation for sufferers from eating disorders. I often think a speaker who has been there and back, so to speak, that is somebody who has experienced one of these conditions and has recovered, may be a much more suitable person than a medical consultant who has never suffered from the condition. However, on the broader front, socio-cultural changes will be necessary before these conditions can be fully defeated. Earlier in the chapter, I adverted to the condemnation of obesity by the western world as being ugly and undesirable. Perhaps it is time for us to reassess our attitudes to slimness and obesity. Perhaps also the fashion world might look at the images they are displaying, but they often tell us that they are simply following public demand. Stress caused by eating disorders, whether they be Anorexia Nervosa, Bulimia Nervosa, binge-eating disorders, compulsive overeating or comfort eating should not be underestimated. As we go into the next millennium maybe it is time for us to take a more balanced and mature view in relation to body size and body image. I have no doubt that this would significantly decrease the incidence of eating disorders, and most of all, considerably reduce the stress caused by these dreadful conditions.

I think it was the Duchess of Windsor who said, 'You can't be too rich or too thin'. Tom Wolfe, in his excellent book, *The Bonfire of the Vanities,* describes some society hostesses in New York as 'social x-rays'. Indeed, looking at the position in the United States, slimness tends to be associated with people in the higher social classes and obesity pervasive among what are called 'blue collar workers'. This is a complete reversal of the situation from about a century ago when a generously proportioned figure was prized among the affluent and the less fortunate were thinner, mainly because of poor nutrition. There is a relatively new organisation in the States called NAAFA (The National Association for the Advancement of Fat Acceptance). These are people who have been yo-yo dieting for many years but have finally accepted that genetically they are rather large and will remain so no matter how much dieting they indulge in. I think this is perhaps an outlook we might introduce to our own culture, for some people.

Having talked to a number of people associated with NAAFA, they are happy, contented people, as they have left the stress of constant dieting and body image dissatisfaction behind them. This is perhaps a rather extreme example but illustrates how some people come to terms with a body image that perhaps does not conform to society's ideal. We all come in various shapes and sizes and it is important to remember that our framework is determined genetically. It is how we view ourselves and our capabilities as well as our limitations that matters in life. Perhaps if we could extend this to a more healthy and mature attitude and outlook toward body weight and body image, we would be a much more contented nation and perhaps a much less stressed one.

6

Stress and Physical Symptoms

by

Dr John Sheehan

Sick people usually attend a doctor. The doctor asks about the person's complaints. The person responds and the doctor may ask a few more questions. A physical examination is then carried out. Sometimes, tests are required. Then a diagnosis is made. A treatment is devised and often a medication prescribed. Usually, the person gets better. It sounds straightforward. But, what happens if the person does not get better?

Research shows that up to 50% of people attending medical out-patient clinics for the first time have no physical disease present. It sounds staggering. Could 50% of the new patients attending medical out-patient clinics have imaginary symptoms? Could so many people have symptoms 'all in their heads'? Are symptoms such as palpitations, dizziness, chest pain, tummy pain, difficulty breathing, pins and needles, diarrhoea or bloating imaginary? Quite definitely not. So, what could cause them? How can the symptoms be explained?

Having attended a doctor, if a person does not get better, he returns to the doctor. More questions are asked, perhaps further tests are arranged and usually the person is given additional or different treatment. Frequently, the doctor reassures the person and offers an explanation for the symptoms. In the main, the explanation and treatment are adequate and the person gets better.

If a person remains ill despite treatments, then often a doctor will refer the person to hospital for a specialist opinion. In cases of emergency, the person may be referred directly to the Accident and Emergency Department where further blood tests, x-rays and assessments are conducted. The person may even be admitted to hospital. Alternatively, the person may be seen as an out-patient. After more tests, a diagnosis is usually made and a treatment prescribed. Again, with specialist input, the person usually gets better. But, not always.

Often, at this stage, the person begins to think that he must have something seriously wrong with him and the doctors will not tell him. The doctors begin to think that the person may have a stress-related condition but are worried that they might have missed a rare disease that might require a very specialised test to discover it. Some doctors say to the patient that there is nothing wrong with them. The patient becomes angry and frustrated. The doctors become frustrated. Both parties can become either defensive or aggressive. The doctor may suggest a second opinion at this stage. The person may decide to see another doctor anyway, perhaps in a different hospital. Sometimes, a well-intentioned family member or friend intervenes and advises on a specific course of action. Visits to alternative or complimentary therapists begin and health food shops are visited. Homeopathic remedies are tried. The person may visit several alternative practitioners while, at the same time, continuing with traditional doctors. All the person wants is to be well.

So, how can the person's symptoms be explained when all the conventional tests are normal? One has to start with the concept of 'illness'. When a person becomes ill, he assumes the 'sick role'. Originally described by Parsons in 1951, the 'sick role' has four components: exemption from normal responsibilities; exemption from responsibility for certain aspects of behaviour; responsibility to try and recover; and responsibility to seek appropriate help. The ill person is therefore not expected to do the things that he normally does, such as work. If the person is irritable or remains in bed all day, it is acceptable as part of being sick. The person must try and recover and this involves using acceptable and recognised methods to do so. For example, if a person has a bad flu, he must keep warm, take hot drinks, not infect others and if necessary, see a doctor.

Everybody knows that physical diseases cause physical symptoms and lead to the 'sick role'. Not many people know that stress can also cause physical symptoms. The physical symptoms caused by stress can be identical to those caused by physical diseases. The following is an example:

A woman in her 50s presented to her family doctor complaining of tummy pain, cramps, bloating and some diarrhoea. The symptoms had been present for about six months and were getting worse. Her doctor examined her and did not find any abnormalities. He sent the woman to the local hospital for some blood tests. The results were all normal. He explained the results to the woman but as her symptoms persisted, he referred her to a specialist for specific tests on her bowel. Extensive investigations were performed and no abnormality was found. The woman was puzzled by her symptoms. Her family doctor then made further inquiries into her symptoms. He asked her about her family. She broke down crying at that stage and informed the doctor that six months previously, her only sister had died with bowel cancer in England. She had been very close to her sister and had no other surviving family. Both her parents had died when she was young.

The case indicates how stressful events can cause physical symptoms. It is likely that stress interacts with several factors to produce the symptoms. The factors include the person's genetic constitution, personality traits, coping skills, previous history and experience of illness and family history of illness. Social factors are also most important and include the person's support from family and friends, work situation, finances and ways in which the person deals with stress.

Stressful events are generally regarded as unpleasant, painful, unhappy or difficult. A family death, losing one's job, major financial debts or serious illness are all obviously stressful. But, can pleasant, happy events be regarded as stressful? The answer is definitely 'Yes'. A wedding is a good example. Described as the happiest day of your life, a wedding can be fraught. Beginning with the preparations, which can be up to several years before the event, the pressure rises with the fixing of a date with the priest or minister, the choosing of a dress, arranging the reception, choosing bridesmaids or groomsmen, writing speeches and so on. It is no wonder that society determined that a couple would have a honeymoon after the event to recover!

Human beings need stress to function. Stress is essentially normal and part of our everyday lives. If one does not have stress in one's life, then one will not be able to work properly, participate successfully in leisure activities or function socially. With too little stress, a person is under-stimulated and bored. We are all probably familiar with the expression that if you want something done then ask a busy person to do it. If one has only one thing to do in a day and the whole day to do it, it is amazing how difficult it becomes to motivate oneself to actually go and do it.

With the optimum amount of stress, a person's life is manageable and balanced. He copes at home and at work, is even-tempered and probably leads a healthy lifestyle. The daily challenges presented to him are dealt with effectively and efficiently and he has a sense of achievement.

When too much stress occurs, a person begins to feel that he is running just to keep still. A sense of being overloaded occurs and the person's performance begins to drop off. Efficiency and effectiveness deteriorate and the person gets less done despite having more to do. Often, time for relaxation is forfeited and the person can become exhausted. If unchecked, too much stress can lead to either a physical or mental breakdown. Signs of excessive stress include drinking too much, smoking extra cigarettes, becoming irritable or narky, not sleeping well or overeating.

A woman in her 30s presented to her doctor complaining of several physical symptoms including palpitations, chest tightness and difficulties speaking. After extensive investigations, no physical cause could be found. She appeared well and had no evidence of depression, anxiety or any other nervous disorder. The symptoms were disabling and interfering with her daily activities. Her family doctor asked her to record a diary detailing when the symptoms occurred, and in particular, what she was doing at the time of the onset of the symptoms. The woman returned a week later with her diary. She had made a startling discovery. Her symptoms began each day when she started to return home. On further questioning, it became clear that the woman had major marital problems and that there was marked tension in the home. In fact, her husband was a domineering man and she was unable to stand up for herself. She said that she felt unable to confront him, particularly as he had quite a temper.

The example quoted above demonstrates how psychological stress can lead to physical symptoms. The woman's symptoms were real but due to psychological stress. The symptoms were not imagined or fictitious.

Social factors may also play a major role in the causation of physical symptoms. It is unclear what the exact mechanism is that converts social problems into symptoms. Several theories exist to explain the relationship but even without knowing the exact mechanism, one sees the effects of social difficulties in clinical practice on a daily basis. The following example illustrates the point:

> *A young, single mother, who had recently given birth to her third child and was living on the sixth floor of a flat complex, presented to her doctor with headaches. She stated that it felt like her head was about to burst. The headaches were present every day and were only partially relieved by paracetamol. Physical examination did not reveal any abnormalities. Her blood pressure was normal. The doctor asked about stress. Further inquiry revealed that the lift in the flat complex where she lived was broken and would not he repaired as heroin addicts had been using it as a place to inject themselves. This meant that the woman had to carry her new baby, the buggy and her shopping up six flights of stairs every day as well as keep charge of her other two older children. The woman's eldest child was four and the second child was two. She added that she would not allow the four-year-old out to play where she lived as dirty needles and syringes were often dumped in the corridors and she was terrified that one of her children would injure themselves with a needle and contract AIDS. The situation was compounded as she was claiming a lone parent's allowance but was cohabiting with her boyfriend and obtaining assistance from him. Officially, he lived at another address but she was unable to cope with her three children without his help. She was also terrified that Social Welfare officers would discover what was happening and take her benefits from her.*

In a study of 96 patients attending a specialist clinic in England for recurrent or persistent abdominal pain, 15 were found to have a physical problem, 31 were suffering from depression, 21 from an anxiety disorder, 17 from a condition called conversion disorder and 12 were alcoholics who had not previously been diagnosed. It is worth exploring these conditions in a little detail.

Depression is a common psychiatric disorder. It is, in fact, as common as heart disease and cancer put together. However, people with depression are not rushed off to hospital with blue lights flashing and sirens blaring and they do not have to attend hospitals for chemotherapy with the possibility of losing their hair. No, depression is often a silent illness that creeps up on an individual causing them to become withdrawn and socially isolated. Friends and neighbours are more likely to think that they have not seen the person recently rather than notice that the person is sick. Most people experience a low mood from time to time. This is not depression in a medical sense. A medical depression, otherwise known as a depressive disorder, lasts at least for many weeks and is pervasive. It is associated with a loss of interest and a loss of enjoyment in activities that are usually pleasurable to an individual. It gives rise to physical complaints in several ways. Physical symptoms can be part and parcel of a depressive disorder. Loss of appetite, weight loss, impaired sleep, fatigue, loss of energy, listlessness, amenorrhoea and loss of interest in sex are all well-recognised as part of a depressive disorder. If a person presents to a doctor with weight loss, the doctor has to consider the main causes of weight loss including cancer and serious physical diseases. If the patient gives a history of low mood, loss of interest and enjoyment, as well as other characteristic symptoms, then a diagnosis of depression is made.

Depressed individuals have negative and pessimistic thoughts. Ordinary bodily sensations that normally would hardly be noticed become sinister when the person is depressed. Sometimes, a person becomes convinced that he has cancer and no amount of persuasion can make him change his mind.

Depression also lowers a person's tolerance so that conditions which the person copes with when well become intolerable when depressed. Arthritis, back pain, chest problems and chronic conditions like diabetes are some examples.

The diagnosis of depression in people with physical symptoms can be difficult as physical illness can also lead to depression. The important question is which came first, the physical symptoms or the depression?

Anxiety disorders can also present with physical symptoms. In generalised anxiety disorder, a person presents with fear, dread, tension or a plethora of physical symptoms that relate to the autonomic nervous system. Common symptoms include palpitations, difficulty breathing or catching one's breath, chest pains, diarrhoea, pins and needles, sweating, dizziness, feeling faint, headache or backache. Often, the person with palpitations will attend a heart specialist, the individual with headaches, a neurologist and the sufferer with diarrhoea, a gastroenterologist. Making the correct diagnosis can be difficult as the patient does not suspect that he has an anxiety disorder and often is extremely worried about the possibility of a very serious physical condition such as multiple sclerosis or in recent times, CJD.

Another anxiety condition called *Panic Disorder* often presents with physical symptoms. The condition is characterised by attacks of physical symptoms associated with thinking that one is about to die or collapse or suffer something dreadful like a stroke. The attacks begin out of the blue and can lead to another condition called *Agoraphobia* if a person begins to avoid specific places like supermarkets because of the panic attacks. Many people with panic disorder initially present to Accident and Emergency Departments as they think that they are having a heart attack.

Conversion disorder is used to describe a situation where a person presents with symptoms and signs of disease but no physical disease is present. Often, the person obtains benefit from being ill and the symptoms can have symbolic significance. It is thought that the symptoms are due to a conflict within the individual but are not expressed in such terms but rather are 'converted' into physical symptoms. For example:

> *A man in his 50s, on holidays with his wife and children, presented to the Accident and Emergency Department of a hospital on a Sunday morning. He stated that he had developed a weakness of his right arm the previous night and was unable to use it. He had never been sick before except for an appendectomy as a child. Physical examination was normal except that the man could not use his right arm. When asked to move it, he could only shake it about a little bit. An emergency CAT-scan of his brain was ordered to exclude the possibility of a stroke. The scan was completely*

normal. Because of his incapacity, he was admitted to hospital. The admitting doctor asked to speak to the man's wife. However, she was not present. It transpired that she had left earlier that morning, returning home with the children. When questioned further, it became clear that the weakness in the arm had developed during a blazing row between the man and his wife. He stated that he had wished to strike her but that he had lost the power in his arm at the time. He had never hit her at any time during the marriage and was ashamed at his intention to hit her. Clearly, the loss of power in his arm had prevented him from acting on his impulse to physically assault his wife. The symptom was produced by the internal conflict between his wish to hit her and his usual self-restraint.

Alcoholism can lead to multiple physical symptoms and ultimately can be fatal. Alcohol has a direct toxic effect on the brain and liver and people who are alcoholic frequently become vitamin deficient which can lead to further problems. Patients presenting with liver disease may minimise their alcohol consumption and deny having a problem with alcohol. With continued drinking, the person develops heart, nerve or brain damage and the damage may be permanent.

In this article, I have attempted to show how stress can lead to physical symptoms. I have taken a broad view of stress and included stressful events, psychological factors, social factors and psychiatric disorders. The management of the symptoms produced by stress essentially includes the treatment of both the symptoms and the causes. If one only treats the symptoms, the symptoms return when the person is re-exposed to the causes.

The woman described who presented with abdominal symptoms precipitated by the death of her only sister required treatment for both her physical and emotional problems. She was prescribed a specific diet by her doctor and given some medication for her diarrhoea. She was also referred to a bereavement counsellor. She returned to health over the ensuing four months. The woman in her 30s who had palpitations, chest tightness and difficulty speaking required assertiveness training. As she grew in confidence, she decided that she had to stand up to her husband. He was initially perplexed and stated that she had changed since he married her. Then, faced with the prospect of losing his marriage or adapting to the new circumstances the husband acceded to his wife's wish that they obtain counselling and they subsequently commenced marital therapy.

The young, single mother with three children, living on the sixth floor of the flat complex was treated with relaxation training for her headaches. A public health nurse arranged a crêche for the two-year-old child and letters were obtained for rehousing. The woman contacted her local T.D. who promised to do all she could for the woman. The headaches improved but did not disappear completely.

Regarding psychiatric disorders, the treatments may be psychological, social or physical. Non-addictive medications may have an important part to play. With correct treatment of depression or anxiety, physical symptoms can melt away and the person is restored to health. Usually, treatment is required for several months.

General measures are very helpful in terms of stress management. Eating a healthy diet, taking exercise, spending time in recreational activities, restricting both alcohol and nicotine consumption and getting adequate sleep are all important. Specific measures such as relaxation exercises, yoga, transcendental meditation, massage and biofeedback are also often helpful. Prayer and involvement in spiritual activities are beneficial to many. Bringing a balance back to one's life is crucial.

Physical symptoms produced by stress cause a person to become ill. Conventionally, illness is regarded as a bad thing. But, if the person can obtain help with the symptoms and accurately identify the causes of the stress, then by addressing the causes, the potential exists for personal growth and development. The individual can emerge a stronger and wiser person, less likely to succumb to further stresses, with improved relationships, tolerance and self-knowledge. The road is often difficult but the potential gains are great.

7

Chronic Fatigue Syndrome

by

Yvonne Tone

'I was 40 years of age, and was always fit and active. I played tennis, swam and enjoyed life to the full. I was back at work having returned after a flu-like illness but still felt feverish, nauseous and dizzy. I struggled for the next four months with low energy, poor concentration and weakness. I felt exhausted all of the time. On my good days I'd try to do too much, telephone home, call to friends in a desperate attempt to feel normal. On my bad days my bed became an unwanted refuge. I even found it difficult to get up to wash my hair. I felt a progressive decline and was unable to articulate in a meaningful way what was happening to me. I went from GP to specialist in an incessant search for relief, but to no avail. I felt my self-sufficiency was gone. I was struggling to climb the stairs at home. I found I needed a wheelchair to face the world and I began to fear the worst. I changed my diet, tried meditation, and all sorts of promised cures as I noted a deterioration from a competent self-sufficient person to someone who could hardly walk across the room. I used to say to myself, 'What is wrong with me? Why can't people understand? Have I too many stresses in my life? Am I suffering from a life-threatening, undetected illness?' It was like a life-sentence. I wondered would I ever recover?'

Feeling tired can be a common problem for people who live full and busy lives. They may complain of feeling drained or lethargic, exhausted or worn-out. This tiredness is in itself not uncommon and is generally transient. It may be viewed as a signal that the body needs rest. When rest is taken, or after a good night's sleep, most people feel re-energised and refreshed and resume their normal activities quite quickly.

In situations where tiredness persists it is reasonable to seek a medical opinion to ascertain its cause. It may be due to a physical illness such as a viral or bacterial infection. It may be due to anaemia or a thyroidal problem. It may also result from psychological stress. Some may describe hectic lifestyles with excessive demands made on them as contributing to its onset. Major personal upheavals can also increase vulnerability to tiredness. Excessive tiredness may result from a combination of physical and psychological factors and the cause is often difficult to pinpoint. If it persists over many months and despite extensive investigations no clear cause has been elicited, it may well be described as Chronic Fatigue.

Chronic Fatigue Syndrome is a condition which is characterised by severe, unexplained, fatigue and exhaustion. This fatigue usually persists for longer than six months and is there for more than 50% of the time. A number of centres around the world are actively engaged in research in this area. The total number of persons with Chronic Fatigue has proved difficult to work out. Studies estimate that between 0.2–1.5% of the population have Chronic Fatigue Syndrome. Most reported cases occur in young to middle-aged adults, with females diagnosed more frequently than males. The cause of Chronic Fatigue is unknown. It is unclear from research whether or not Chronic Fatigue is a single illness or a group of different illnesses that share common symptoms. Some causative theories focus on an underlying viral infection, while others focus on possible underlying immunological, hormonal or psychological dysfunction. Some people may also refer to this condition as Myalgic Encephalomyelitis, Post-Viral Fatigue Syndrome, Yuppie flu, or Chronic Fatigue Immune Dysfunction Syndrome. Chronic Fatigue Syndrome is a useful descriptive term that does not imply any one specific cause in describing this complex condition and is accepted by most practitioners.

The symptoms experienced by somebody presenting with Chronic Fatigue can vary. Many may report a 'flu-like' illness at its onset. They may commonly complain of severe tiredness or exhaustion which is not relieved by rest and which they describe as different from 'normal' tiredness. This tiredness may be accompanied by a range of other unpleasant symptoms such as muscle and/or joint pain, headaches, dizziness and sore throat. People may also describe feeling mentally fatigued and complain that their concentration is affected. They may also experience memory difficulties or find it hard to keep conversations going.

Disruption in normal sleeping habits is also commonly described. Some people report difficulty getting to sleep or may wake frequently during the night. They may find that sleep is no longer refreshing. The consequences of a disrupted sleep pattern are irritability, an increase in fatigue symptoms and an inability to carry out normal routine activities. In order to cope with this, some people may take naps during the day to catch up on sleep missed, others sleep for 12–16 hours at night. Most will say that fatigue is increased by carrying out everyday activities and it is easy for them then to find their lives becoming restricted. In some cases, after a long period of time, they may become bed-bound or feel the necessity to use a wheelchair intermittently.

Chronic Fatigue is a stressful condition. Besides experiencing the above symptoms those affected often feel misunderstood by others or find their illness may not be taken seriously. Many will have sought medical advice and will have been extensively investigated. The results of these investigations may not reveal any significant abnormality or offer an explanation as to the cause of the fatigue problem. This can be frustrating and upsetting to the sufferer in their quest for a solution to their problem.

> *'I remember meeting a work colleague on the way home from the doctor's surgery having been told further tests were negative. He looked at me in surprise telling me how well I looked. I struggled to explain that despite the fact I looked well, I didn't feel well. I felt a desperate need to be understood and for a fleeting moment thought it would have been easier to say I had cancer.'*

A further effect of the elusive cause of this illness is that sufferers may not be able to receive any really effective treatment from their General Practitioner. It is not surprising that, frustrated with this situation, many turn to the alternative medicine sector in a relentless search for relief. While this may help to some degree in some instances, it may also create a continuous financial drain on resources without effecting a cure. It is always important to remember that Chronic Fatigue is a complex condition and a cautious approach is needed, particularly if someone promises an instant cure.

Chronic Fatigue is not only stressful for the patients themselves, but also for their families and friends. It is difficult for families to watch someone they care for struggle with the fluctuating effects of this condition and the limits it puts on their lives. Some families may cope by adjusting their lifestyles and go to extraordinary lengths to accommodate changes brought about by the illness. Family members are also stressed by being unable to know how best to help their loved one. They want to provide support and understanding but are unsure as to whether they should be encouraging or discouraging. They can feel drawn into doing more and more for the person who is ill and yet may feel uneasy that they are fostering a dependence.

> *'My legs felt heavy. I could hardly walk across the room. I supported myself by holding on to furniture strategically placed to allow me the freedom of my home. I watched TV for half-an-hour and then rested to conserve my energy as a friend was due to call. My friends were so important. Why did I tire so easily? The limits on my life were frightening. Every time I did a simple task I had to take more and more rest to conserve what little energy I believed I had.'*

As the cause of most Chronic Fatigue is often unclear it is important to focus on a range of factors that can play a part in this condition. People react to the symptoms they experience in different ways in an effort to overcome their persistent feeling of tiredness. Some will take more rest in the hope of improvement. Others may carry out vigorous exercise on the days they feel better in the hope that they can beat the problem in this way. The result of this inconsistent approach is that doing too much one day leads to exhaustion, and doing too little for several days leads to more tiredness and feelings of demoralisation. Because of sporadic efforts trying to overcome the symptoms, muscular aches and pains are then made worse and people begin to worry they may have caused permanent damage to their muscles by pushing themselves too hard. It is natural that if they have experience of this pattern of activity and rest, with a resultant increase in physical symptoms, they may then find themselves thinking in quite a negative or unhelpful way. They may think they are worse because they have engaged in activity which has resulted in more fatigue. This is an understandable reaction because in the initial stages of any illness it is usually advisable to rest for a short period. Therefore, it is common to experience an initial increase in symptoms, bearing in mind their previous lengthy inactivity. Subsequently, people may describe feeling fatigued on exertion or re-engaging in sports or strenuous daily activity. As a result, they may then reduce their activity further which leads to feelings of hopelessness and frustration. Because the symptoms are experienced at increasingly lower levels of exercise, being active becomes more of a strain. Gradually, they then become engaged in a vicious circle of activity and rest as they endeavour to manage their illness in these two ways.

Naturally, this inability to function in the same way as before their illness contributes to a pattern of negative thinking. They may think: 'I must still be really ill because I'm not able to do that simple task. Perhaps I need a few more days rest'. Often people will attribute their increase in symptoms to a recurrence of a virus or a bacterial infection as the source of their symptoms, instead of attributing it to their lowered level of fitness.

If this pattern persists over time they become enmeshed in a circle of increasing avoidance, more inactivity and more fatigue as a result. Due to the persistent and chronic nature of the condition, it is easy to understand that people may experience tearfulness, reduced energy and motivation and become unable to enjoy life as before.

In many cases people may describe feeling depressed because of their circumstances, which is an understandable response to what is happening in their lives. This often increases their stress because of fears that their problem may then be viewed as purely psychological. Some psychiatrists may use antidepressants for the treatment of specific symptoms. The physical symptoms experienced in response to psychological stress are real and not imagined. It is useful to remember that experiencing depression is not a sign of weakness but merely a human response to stress. In the majority of cases Chronic Fatigue Syndrome clearly involves physical symptoms in addition to psychological effects and treatment should be holistic in its approach to be effective.

'I was really dismayed when I went for help that I was asked about life before my illness. What had work, relationships, family or life stresses to do with my physical symptoms? I gradually realised it was difficult to separate my illness in the black and white way I viewed my situation. Over time I became more comfortable talking about issues I had previously viewed as unimportant. This was helpful to me in addition to describing my physical symptoms.'

It is evident that Chronic Fatigue is a complex condition with multi-factorial causes that persist over a prolonged time period. Many people recognise the power the mind has in influencing the body. Commonly, people try to divide the mind from the body, when it is evident they are intertwined; physically when people feel at a low ebb their moods can be affected, similarly if over-stressed they may be more prone to physical illness. There is often a reluctance to acknowledge the role thoughts and emotions play in the state of health and illness.

The first important consideration in managing any illness, and Chronic Fatigue is no different, is that those affected be given a reasonable explanation as to what may be going wrong. It is important they have some understanding as to why they feel fatigued and so unwell. This may involve exploring, precipitating and maintaining factors in addition to assessing each individual's response. There is often a reluctance to acknowledge the role that thoughts and emotions play in determining the state of health and illness. Faced with this debilitating condition it may also involve looking at how they are coping at the moment with their symptoms. Because of prolonged periods of inactivity, physiotherapy and massage therapy may help in gradually increasing levels of fitness.

It is always helpful to encourage people to break down their illness experience into several manageable phases rather than engage in an overwhelming assault on all its aspects. The person affected needs to understand that their illness is determined by many different factors – physiological changes, changes in mood and thought processes and reactions of other people to them. The rationale is that they can be helped but only if they are prepared to participate by taking an active role in the treatment process aimed at re-shaping their lives. This approach may well be seen as different from other approaches they may have experienced. At this stage a person may feel, having been ill for a long time, that they have tried everything and done everything to help themselves. Whilst this may be true to some degree, the problem is not what they have tried to do, but how they have gone about it.

Despite the fact that a specific cause of the fatigue state may be unclear it is possible to teach people how to manage their symptoms. It is important to encourage the person affected to engage in a treatment approach aimed at reducing the effects of the illness and to focus on rehabilitation. One such treatment approach is Cognitive Behavioural Therapy, which can be helpful in improving symptoms and quality of life.

The main goal of a cognitive behavioural approach is to enhance self-control and resourcefulness and to reduce demoralisation. It is of most value to those who accept that Chronic Fatigue is a complex problem with presenting features involving physical and psychological symptoms. Treatment is aimed at giving instruction on some strategies that may reduce stress and enhance coping skills in an effort to improve their quality of life. Simon Wessley and his team at the Institute of Psychiatry, London, have devised a cognitive behavioural approach aimed at breaking what they describe as this vicious circle of fatigue. They have put forward the view that an initial virus may cause different responses in an individual, such as fatigue and muscle pain, inactivity or depressive feelings. If this persists over time, it can trigger a further increase in symptoms, including further demoralisation and further fatigue.

Treatment starts by working towards breaking the link between fatigue symptoms and stopping or reducing activity. This is done by engaging the person to start with a carefully-planned, mutually agreed programme of graded, consistent activity with planned rest periods. These rest periods should be taken even though they may feel they are not needed in the initial stages. The aim of this graded exercise programme is to help build up physical strength and gradually increase the amount of activity that can be comfortably managed over time.

The cognitive element of this approach involves looking at how thoughts can influence behaviour in maintaining inactivity and avoidance behaviour. Thoughts are important because sometimes they interfere with the ability to do things. Negative thinking patterns can exist unrecognised. It is useful to examine the way people look at things and how their interpretations may influence their behaviour. A powerful way of controlling and questioning these thoughts is to learn to identify them and challenge those that are unrealistic and unhelpful. This can be difficult as these thoughts tend to be automatic and so are hard to control. It may seem reasonable to believe these thoughts despite the fact that they may be inaccurate, because they seem to be logical. A typical example might be:

'If I arrange to go out on Friday evening I know I'll be tired, so I better rest all day Thursday in preparation.'

It is important to become aware of these thoughts and learn how to identify them. This can be achieved through self-monitoring, by writing these thoughts in diary form.

There are typical thinking errors identified by many health professionals who use cognitive techniques. Those who engage in these thinking errors can distort reality. The following table, based on thinking errors identified by the American psychiatrist, Aaron T. Beck, shows some examples of this:

Negative thought	Description	Example
All-or-nothing thinking.	Looking at things in black or white categories.	I'm useless, I've tried everything. I'll never get better.
Over-generalization.	You see a single negative event as a never-ending pattern of defeat.	I got up yesterday and felt tired– this increased activity will never work.
Disqualifying the positive.	You reject positive experience by insisting it doesn't count.	So what if I'm a bit better today, I bet I'll be worse by the weekend.
Catastrophising.	You get things out of proportion.	I feel worse today, I bet I've done myself more harm.
'Should' statements.	You make unrealistic rules of living.	I should be feeling better.

Having identified these thoughts it is then important to find what alternative views are available. For example:

'I went out three weeks ago without resting the day before with no ill-effect. Perhaps I need not rest all day Thursday.'

It is very useful to write out alternative thoughts despite initial difficulties believing them. Challenging negative thinking and coming up with reasonable alternatives takes practice. It involves examining the basic assumptions or 'rules of living' we have and looking at the meaning these have for us. It is approached in a questioning way by asking: 'What evidence have I for thinking this way? How helpful is it to think in this manner? What are the advantages and disadvantages of thinking in this way?' It means being able to make links between thoughts and behaviour. It is best done in written form and in a systematic way to be useful. It can be extremely useful because it allows people the ability to get to know what they are doing, and how they are feeling emotionally, at the time they engage in negative thinking. The aim of examining thoughts more closely and generating alternative ways of viewing things is to help people feel better. It is useful to be able to control these thoughts in a reasonable way because of the powerful way they can influence behaviour.

A cognitive behavioural approach involves looking at resources people may not be aware they have and using their abilities in a much more structured way. It will only be helpful with continued efforts over time to put it to use. It means learning more about the precipitating and maintaining factors of the illness and using this knowledge to build a plan to address these. It is helpful to work, if possible, with someone who can understand and work with you using this approach. This may be a General Practitioner, a psychologist, a psychiatrist, a counsellor or a behavioural psychotherapist.

Self-management is also useful and would involve the following guidelines:

1. Monitor your daily activities and rest periods over two to three days. This self-monitoring will help you establish a baseline from which you can then plan the next stage of treatment. Use a simple scale to monitor your level of fatigue at intervals during the day.

Activity Chart Using a Fatigue Scale

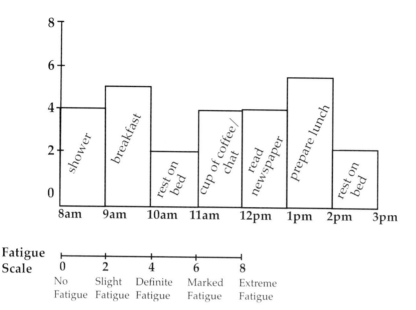

Record all activity no matter how trivial it may seem. This will help identify patterns and generate ideas for easy goals. An advantage of self-monitoring is that it can be encouraging to look back at the chart and see what progress you are making.

2. Accept that if you have been physically inactive for a long time, it is natural that when you engage in a graded exercise programme you will experience an initial increase in fatigue and perhaps an increase in muscle pain. Such symptoms should reduce after a few days. As you make progress, remind yourself you have been ill for a long time. Gradual, consistent progress is better in the long-run. Avoid engaging in over-activity when you have 'a good day'. It is better to be successful at small goals than to be disappointed if you try to do too much.

Set goals that are realistic and achievable. Depending on what level you're at, an example may be 'to sit out for five minutes morning, afternoon, and evening' or, if you are more active, it may be 'to walk for 20 minutes twice daily'. Persist with the same goals for seven to ten days until you feel you are more comfortable in achieving them. Gradually increase further in a consistent way.

3. Be aware of the power of negative thinking and how it can contribute to increases in physiological arousal. Use positive self-coping statements such as, 'I may feel tired now, but I am increasing my activity, so this is reasonable. Next week I won't feel quite as tired'. It may be useful to write these thoughts down in diary form or construct an activity chart as described previously.

4. Try to reduce symptom hypervigilance. Sometimes, a person can become preoccupied with how they are feeling physically. If we can occupy our minds with other things the intensity of symptoms can lessen. Distraction can help by allowing us to be absorbed in something which may help us notice symptoms less.

5. Allow yourself periods of relaxation. This may involve yoga, meditation, listening to tapes or reading. It may also be helpful to have massage or low-key physiotherapy exercises aimed at improving circulation, decreasing muscle pain and increasing fitness.

6. Remember:

    (a) Activity should only be gradually increased.
    (b) Start with a simple task and build on this slowly and consistently.
    (c) Undertake this activity for short periods of time initially.
    (d) Practice goals regularly and consistently.
    (e) Do not be put off if fatigue increases initially. This is normal.
    (f) Setbacks may be experienced – do not let these put you off.
    (g) Bear in mind that this approach is one of rehabilitation. It will take time. It may help you overcome symptoms of an illness that has been there, perhaps for a long time.
    (h) Give yourself credit for goals achieved, no matter how small. Share your successes with others and enjoy their encouragement.

A cognitive behavioural approach can work by helping people discover the most useful ways of managing and hopefully overcoming this stressful illness by focusing on how it affects their thoughts, feelings and behaviour. It is not an instant cure and its approach is primarily one of rehabilitation. It has been our experience, and also the experiences of others, that it does help some people to improve their quality of life, and with time, recover from their illness.

8

Stress and Alcohol Dependence

by

Rolande Anderson

'I could murder a pint', 'One for the road', 'A drink to relax' – all familiar, comfortable, everyday expressions relating to our use of alcohol. Does alcohol help us to unwind or reduce stress? The answer depends on the individual responding to the question. For most people social drinking is just a way of socialising, a method of relaxation, a time to deprogramme from the stresses and strains of everyday living. For those who are dependent on alcohol, it only adds to the stresses of everyday life and can ultimately destroy their very existence.

Stress reduction has become the preoccupation of the modern generation. Ever-increasing consumer, work, financial, domestic and life pressures have led to the development of a whole range of weird and wonderful therapies and strategies to take away the worries and concerns of day-to-day living. We live in an instant society, where we can get almost anything immediately – fast foods and instant replays, to name but a few. Not surprising in this secular, consumer society, instant highs and instant solutions to emotional pain are also actively sought and pursued.

Enter onto the stage the drugs of addiction, many of them 'man made' instant cures, developed, purchased and consumed for the quick fix – painkillers, ecstasy, hallucinogens. They are all aptly named – in the short-term. All of them peddle an instant 'hit' with no hint of the danger in the long-term. All of them offer immediate relief and pleasure. Alongside these modern drugs exists the old Irish favourite – alcohol, or more correctly, the drug ethyl alcohol, which is still the most commonly abused drug of all in our society. It is used happily and healthily by the vast majority of people, but can cause significant problems for heavy drinkers or moderate users. It also causes dependence and desolation among those who become addicted and among their families.

Varying estimates suggest that 6-18% of drinkers could be alcohol dependent. Alcohol has been there since time began and it is ever-present in our society and available at most, if not all of the important life stages and events – christenings, birthdays, debs dances, office parties, business lunches, sporting occasions, festive events, marriages and deaths. 'Drowning our sorrows', 'Celebrating our successes', 'Going out with a bang', 'Numbing the pain' – all of these are well-known phrases. In fact, what alcohol does is bury our feelings, when used to excess.

Alcohol Dependence Syndrome, which is categorised as a disease by the World Health Organisation, is more commonly known as Alcoholism. A useful definition might be to describe the condition as one where the drinking causes a continuing and/or progressive interference in any area of the life of the individual. Unfortunately, there is no simple medical test to determine the existence of Alcohol Dependence Syndrome and a detailed clinical assessment is needed to determine the condition. This process involves an assessment of the person's biological, psychological, social, emotional and spiritual well-being. There is an ongoing controversy regarding the use of the term *Disease* as opposed to the term *Addiction*. This public debate adds little to the suffering of the victims of the condition and, sadly, has been used by some to cut or reduce spending on treatment facilities. However, whether alcohol dependence is a disease of addiction or an addictive disease, a syndrome or a condition doesn't really matter. What matters is that the individual alcoholic, once diagnosed, takes responsibility for recovery.

Development of Alcohol Dependence Syndrome is usually quite subtle, although some alcoholics say and believe that they were alcoholic almost from the very first drink. Why do some people develop this condition and others do not? Most writers on the subject describe the causation as multi-factorial, usually involving a complex mix of factors such as heredity, biology, life-events, family background, social and cultural determinants, and personality. Some have also shown quite conclusively a strong link between mood disorders and alcohol dependence, which is not surprising considering the mood-altering effect usually sought by the individual who becomes dependent on alcohol. Many people who suffer from clinical depression and who are consequently stressed out, turn to alcohol for its short-term, self-medicating effects. Unfortunately, because alcohol is a depressant, in the majority of cases this will only make the depression worse in the long-term and also carries the risk of dependence for the individuals concerned.

There is also a strong connection between the use of alcohol to reduce anxiety and a whole range of phobias, particularly social phobia – the fear of meeting people. While we must be careful, of course, to avoid simple explanations, nevertheless, in all of the above factors, the common theme is the attempted avoidance of discomfort, stress and pain. A distinction must also be made between why someone starts to drink abusively and why someone continues to drink in an addictive manner. There are a million reasons for the former, but only one for the latter, namely Alcohol Dependence Syndrome. The wise old saying is very apt: 'Man takes a drink, drink takes a drink, drink takes the man'. The same applies to women, as we will discuss later. The great paradox is that individuals who start off drinking excessively to cure or to sort out personal problems often end up with the problems unsolved and with a dependency on alcohol into the bargain. This is equally true of any drug of addiction.

Denial is the lifeblood of alcohol dependence. The development of this psychological defence mechanism is also often very subtle. This author believes, however, that a significant number of people who become alcoholic have often experienced denial in other forms in their formative years. For example, in living with the stress at home of coping with an alcoholic father, the child can witness reality being ignored or distorted by both the alcoholic father and also typically by the codependent partner who tries to protect the children from the adverse consequences. 'Your dad was not drunk last night', 'He walked into a door', 'Things will be better next week', 'I can get him to stop', may all be examples of denial at work. Given such circumstances, it would be reasonable to assume that some children might already be programmed for denial.

Denial becomes all-pervasive in the individual alcoholic's life. At the height of the addiction, the individual becomes totally self-absorbed and everything else is ignored and/or neglected. Telling lies, deceit, minimisation, avoidance of subjects or meetings, the use of aggression including angry silences, are all aspects of denial – all of which add to the misery of the alcoholic and their loved ones. Denial becomes necessary, progressive and automatic. Far from relieving stress the individual is consumed by it. The only way to avoid such painful feelings and to get relief is to use the very stuff which contributed to the problems in the first place. In this way the loop of addiction is subtly but ever more firmly established – stress results from the consequences of the use of alcohol, alcohol is used to avoid that stress, further stress is caused, more alcohol is used to avoid the pain of the previous episode, and so on. Such loops can continue uninterrupted for years and may only be halted by the development of a crisis which leads to a resolution.

The signs and symptoms of Alcohol Dependence Syndrome are many and varied – no two alcoholics are exactly alike in presentation. Central to an understanding of alcohol dependence is the question of compulsion, the need to consume drink or a craving for alcohol. Compulsion can be both physical and psychological. A most extreme example of this is the individual alcoholic who, in an attempt to deal with a hangover, needs to get to an 'early house' as quickly as possible. One person told me of his daily bus journey (on the first bus into town) where every bump would rattle his already shaking torso. On reaching his destination, he would have to lean over to put his lips to the glass or use a tie or a belt to lift the glass, such was the unsteadiness of his hands. A female alcoholic told me how she would try to space out her drinking during the day in an attempt to control it:

> *The first one at 8 a.m. and then I would try to wait until 12 for the next – go for a walk and leave it until three o'clock before finally drinking without reference to the clock until fitful sleeping took over. The obsession with time was a nightmare. I would always make sure the blinds were drawn, the phone off the hook, the car parked around the back.'*

What a tortured, stress-filled existence!

Early morning drinking, loss of control, compulsions, drinking to avoid withdrawal symptoms (such as hand tremors) are all signs and symptoms of alcohol dependence. Preoccupation with alcohol, blackouts (memory loss), secret drinking, solitary drinking, the use of excuses and other defence mechanisms also constitute further signs and symptoms. Gulping alcohol to raise the blood alcohol level quickly, going on binges and bouts, a deterioration in the person's appearance and physical well-being, minor and major accidents, psychosomatic complaints, severe difficulties at home and at work and changes in tolerance for alcohol may all be significant signs of a progression towards alcohol dependence. The presence of such signs and symptoms makes for a stress-filled life.

The amount of alcohol that a person drinks usually is not an accurate criterion for the diagnosis; however, the more alcohol an individual drinks, the more he or she is at risk. The Royal College of Psychiatrists in Britain has stated that up to 21 units of alcohol per week for men and 14 units of alcohol per week for women represent safe limits of drinking, although these amounts should be consistent over a period of time and the whole quota should not be consumed at the one time but should be evenly spread over the week. One unit of alcohol roughly equals a half pint of beer or 1 standard measure of other forms of alcohol.

Because of their physical make-up, woman and girls are disadvantaged in relation to men and boys as regards the amount of alcohol their bodies can tolerate and they are also disadvantaged in relation to the negative consequences of alcohol dependence. Female alcoholics tend to suffer from all the alcohol-related medical complications more severely and with more fatal consequences than their male counterparts. With specific reference to the female biological system and stress, many writers in this field have suggested a causative link between the use of alcohol to relieve premenstrual tension and dependency. This connection is tenuous, to say the least. Interestingly and paradoxically, many women in recovery from alcohol dependence who have had such problems claim that there is a substantial reduction in symptoms once sobriety has been maintained for six months or more. If this is indeed a trend it may be directly attributable to sobriety and/or to the consequent improvement in women's physical and mental health. Once again, we see the paradox that the use of alcohol to relieve any kind of stress, tension or pain can, in fact, lead to a marked increase in stress, tension and pain and such usage can also possibly contribute to dependency.

The impact of alcohol dependence on the family deserves special mention and attention. Those who live with or are involved in a relationship with someone who is dependent on alcohol often complain of being 'stressed out'. One client, now aged 28, described the stress of living with alcoholism as a child as follows:

> *'We never knew when he (Dad) would come home drunk or when he would be in bad form, but I can remember vividly one evening of sheer terror when he came home. He barged through the front door and had a major row with Ma. One of my brothers stood between them, he threatened to kill her. I wet myself with fear. He soon turned his attention to me. I was cuddling a doll. With a sudden movement he grabbed it and threw it into the fire, saying I should grow up and not be so childish... I was four, for God's sake!*
>
> *This sort of scene was a regular occurrence. Next day I would go to school tired and worn out, my fingernails bitten to the bone. I could never concentrate at school and always felt different. I remember looking at the other kids' dads and wishing they were mine.'*

Obviously, someone living in such circumstances has enormous problems coping with daily living. I remember once getting a call from a boy who turned out to be aged eleven. In a calm, detached, mature voice he rang to see if the hospital had a bed for his mum. He said that his parents were separated and that he had come home from school to find his mother 'blacked out' on the floor. He had already rung the GP, but he was not unduly worried about her as she was just 'drunk as usual.' He had arranged for two younger siblings to go next door so they wouldn't see his mother in such a state and he was able to quote her V.H.I. number. All this at age eleven — a child behaving as an adult, deprived of innocence and fun! Another example might further emphasise this point. A middle-aged alcoholic told me how he had 'conked out' on the settee, only to awaken to the smell of cooking and discover his eight-year-old son with the deep-fat frier on full, a can of peas open and the kettle boiling in an attempt to feed the two younger children aged three and eighteen months!

Uncertainty, lack of consistency and unreliability are the daily diet of those living with someone who is actively addicted. Often frozen with fear and struggling to cope with a sense of failure, they also bottle up their emotions and try to contain the problem without involving outsiders. The immediate partner has all sorts of emotional and practical difficulties to contend with and usually feels an extra burden of responsibility for the health and well-being of the children. In many cases they have to deal with little or no money, little or no support, little or no sleep and a sense of futility. Most are subject to disrespect, silence, verbal abuse. Some also have to deal with physical violence, infidelity and sexual difficulties. One can only wonder and guess how many are 'treated' by GPs, psychologists, social workers, hospital physicians for a range of symptoms of stress-related conditions without the 'real' cause of their problems ever being properly addressed.

One middle-aged woman who was married to someone who had been treated eight or nine times in three or four different treatment agencies without success, said to me:

> 'Nobody really knows what it's like. You hope against hope that things will be different. If he once stopped for good everything would be fine. Your whole life depends on what mood he is in. If he is in good form, I'm in good form; if he's not I'm constantly on edge, worried sick, waiting for the next crisis or outburst.'

Most alcohol/addiction counsellors get referrals from individuals such as this who start by asking: 'How can I get my husband (wife, partner) better?', 'How can I make him/her stop drinking?' The honest answer is that this is impossible and instead the counselling should be geared towards helping partners to recognise and focus on their own needs and to see how they can improve their own situation. These partners/spouses are often in such a state after living in an abusive relationship for some time that they find it almost impossible to talk about themselves without reference to their partner. They lose their own identity and become, for example, the wife of the alcoholic rather than a person in their own right.

'One-to-one' counselling can help a great deal as can involvement in a spouses' or concerned persons' group such as those we have been running in St. Patrick's Hospital in Dublin for the past eighteen years or so. Al-Anon is also a vital self-help group for adult family members. In such groups the 'concerned persons' learn that they are not alone and that others are in the same emotional state and operating and coping with a similar mind-set. Gradually, when encouraged to talk and open up over a period of weeks or even months, they can manage to focus on their own recovery. Despite what has been written, the goal of the therapist at all times should be the recovery of the whole family, whenever this is even remotely possible. Unfortunately, some partners also have to cope with the stresses and strains of separation, a process which adds to the great pressures they have already endured, especially if the costly and emotionally taxing legal system is involved. Al-Ateen, for the teenage children of alcoholics, and Adult Children of Alcoholics, a support group which recognises the long-term negative emotional consequences for children, are also most useful self-help groups.

Alcohol dependence puts extra stress, too, on workmates and employers. Absenteeism, accidents at work, being late for work, increased casual leave, are all consequences of alcohol dependence in the workplace. Misplaced fear and protection of the individual with an alcohol problem by a colleague can or may lead to an increase in frustration, anger, and intolerable stress for colleagues who ultimately and unknowingly enable their addicted workmate to progress towards self-destruction. It is gratifying nowadays to see so many industries and other large employers taking positive action by providing treatment for employees, training for supervisors and other preventive measures. Increasing numbers of people are getting early help from such Employee Assistance Programmes (EAPs) and other long-sighted methods of dealing with the problem. Avoidance of the old methods of sacking, ignoring or transferring should be encouraged at every level. Incidentally, many EAPs cater for other problems that manifest themselves at work including stress management and prevention.

It has been said that for every alcoholic there are three or four other people who are directly, adversely affected, but this must be a gross underestimation. It is definitely true, however, that the person most severely affected is the individual alcoholic. Residential treatment is necessary for a large number of cases and usually treatment results from the inevitable crisis in the person's life. Jeff, a 20-year-old said:

I was drinking since the age of 13. My first drink was a cider with a group of lads from school in a field near my home. I was painfully shy, I'd go red in company and was a bit tongue-tied, and I always felt my family were a bit odd. That first drink made me feel great and I lost my inhibitions. I was accepted as one of the lads. I knew from a very early stage that I had a problem with booze

*but I didn't really care ... and I didn't know what to do
to stop. My drinking progressed to the point where I
couldn't function without it. I used to make all sorts of
promises to myself ... I'll just have one. But when out, I
simply couldn't stop. At some stage I became paranoid
after a few drinks and became really aggressive ...
Someone would say something in a pub that was
probably quite innocent, but I was sure they were
talking about me – and I'd pick a fight. It's incredible,
'cos I wouldn't normally hurt a fly. The crisis really
came for me when on one drunken orgy, I hit my
girlfriend. With the crazy guilt in my head over this, I
drank more and more and smashed the windscreens of
ten or twelve cars on my way home'.*

Another young man, aged 23, came to treatment after a series of
unhappy incidents. 'I knew I had a problem for years because I used
to wet the bed after a heavy session and would wash the sheets
before my folks found out. The real crunch came, however, when one
winter's night, I found myself drinking alone in a strange pub and
some time later woke up on a seat in the Phoenix Park. I had no idea
how I got there. A short while later a German tourist was murdered
near the spot and I remember thinking how lucky I was'. Both these
young men admitted themselves for treatment shortly after these
events.

Successful treatment requires really hard work. Abstinence,
although it is essential in my opinion, is only the start. For a successful
outcome to treatment there has to be a change in attitudes and
behaviour. There are four stages: an awareness of the need to change;
a decision to change; the change in attitude and behaviour itself; and
perhaps most importantly a maintenance and ongoing review of the
change that is necessary. Some individuals need detoxification
followed by a course of treatment involving lectures and counselling
('one-to-one' and groups). In groups, the individuals identify with
others and begin to get hope that recovery is possible.

Letting go of alcohol is a frightening prospect for most alcoholics
as it had seemed like a friend. After the intensive phase of treatment,
after-care is essential and should continue for at least a year. It takes
a long, long time for the person's full confidence to return and for
trust to be re-established in relationships both within and outside the

family. Yet, even after some early months of recovery, the quality of life can improve dramatically. So, while treatment is often very stressful, herein lies another paradox. Successful treatment for the individual alcoholic and their family, though very painful in the short-term, does offer long-term relief. This is in contrast to the short-term gains from alcohol for the dependant individual as already described. Ultimately, treatment is about gaining or regaining the ability to lead a contented life with peace of mind. The most important message is that recovery is possible and can be achieved.

The bottom line is that alcohol does not remove any kind of stress including physical and emotional pain, but may simply numb it for a while. For those who are actively alcohol dependent and their loved ones, alcohol far from relieving stress, results in a life full of stress.

9

Stress and Migraine

by

Elizabeth Lawlor

Migraine is a unique headache syndrome characterised by an excruciating, pulsating pain associated with nausea, vomiting, sensitivity to light *(photophobia)* and sensitivity to noise *(phonophobia)*. The word migraine is derived from the Greek word *hemicrania*. Although *hemicrania* literally means only half the head, migraine involves both sides of the head from its onset in about 40% of patients. Another 40% experience strictly unilateral headaches, and approximately 20% start on one side and later become generalised. Ironically, headache is never the sole feature of migraine. The symptoms of migraine vary to such an extent, from one patient to another and even between recurrent attacks in the same patient, that the strict definition of migraine has always presented difficulties.

The Headache Classification Committee of the International Headache Society, provides the following diagnostic criteria for migraine headache: the person must have had five or more attacks of headache lasting 4 – 72 hours if untreated, with at least two of four features (unilaterality, pulsating quality, moderate or severe intensity, and aggravation by exertion), as well as nausea, with or without vomiting, or *photophobia* and *phonophobia*. Structural abnormalities or other causative lesions should have been excluded by the history, physical examination or, when indicated, by appropriate investigations. According to their classification schemes the two most common types of migraine are *Classic* and *Common*. In *Classic Migraine*, the headache is preceded by an 'aura' which usually consists of visual disturbances (but may involve the other senses). *Common Migraine* has no aura.

Migraine attacks may be divided into five phases:

(1) The *prodrome*, which occurs hours or days before the headache in approximately 60% of migraines, includes psychologic, neurologic, constitutional, and autonomic features. Psychologic symptoms include depression, euphoria, irritability, restlessness, mental slowness, hyperactivity, fatigue and drowsiness. Neurologic phenomena include photophobia, phonophobia and hypersomnia (sleeping a lot). Constitutional symptoms include a stiff neck, a cold feeling, sluggishness, increased thirst, increased urination, anorexia, diarrhoea, constipation, fluid retention and food cravings.

(2) The *aura* which comes immediately before the headache itself, can be characterised by visual, sensory (e.g. pins and needles) or motor phenomena (clumsiness), and may also involve language disturbances (e.g. slurred speech).

(3) The *headache* itself, if it occurs at all, can occur at any time of day or night. The onset is usually gradual; the pain peaks and then subsides, lasting usually between 4 – 72 hours in adults and 2 –48 hours in children. The pain is commonly aggravated by physical activity or simple head movement. Many patients seek out a dark, quiet room. Other symptoms include blurring of vision, nasal stuffiness, anorexia (loss of appetite), hunger, tinnitus (ringing in the ears), diarrhoea, abdominal cramps, polyuria (producing large amounts of urine), pale complexion, sensations of heat or cold and sweating. Impaired concentration is common and light-headedness with a feeling of faintness may occur.

(4) The *headache termination.*

(5) *Postdrome:* Following the headache, the pain wanes and the person may feel tired, washed out, irritable, and listless and may have impaired concentration, scalp tenderness, or mood changes. Some people feel unusually refreshed or euphoric after an attack, whereas others note depression and vague feelings of discomfort.

The exact cause of Migraine is poorly understood, although researchers have made some progress in understanding what happens during an attack. Medical scans have been used to examine the changes in the human brain during spontaneous Migraine attacks. During the attacks, increased blood flow was found in the right or left side of the brain (cerebral hemispheres) and in the brainstem.

The *Migraine Aura* is a very disturbing phenomenon for those migraineurs who experience it (between 20–40% of all migraines). Auras may involve strong feelings of dizziness, sensitivity to and avoidance of bright lights (particularly fluorescent lights), tingling sensations or pins and needles on one side of the body. Some people may experience blindness in part of the visual field, with the border of the blindness characterised by jagged flashing lights. Typically, migraine visual aura consists of poorly localised luminous hallucinations of formless flashes of white or multicoloured lights (photopsias), or zig-zag patterns, wavy lines, heat flashes, or spots or stars seen in the central portion of the visual field. The aura may also be a distinct perception of a central or paracentral blind spot (scotoma), edged by an arc of shiny, shimmering, crenallated shapes which taken together constitute a scintillating scotoma. Like the headache associated with it, the scintillating scotoma is usually unilateral and is seen in the corresponding visual fields. The current characterisation of the migraine aura that is available in the scientific literature is as follows:

(1) There is a lowering of the threshold of excitability of brain cells — in other words, the excitatory cells of the brain fire more easily.

(2) The firing becomes synchronised across a reasonably large area of one side of the brain.

(3) This firing is characterised as an electrical wave which advances across the surface of the brain. At the leading edge of the wave is an area of intense but transient firing of brain cells (hyperexcitability) which is followed by an area of sustained and very depressed activity where brain cells do not fire as often (hypoexcitability). This phenomenon has been labelled 'cortical spreading depression'.

(4) As the 'spreading depression' invades different brain areas concerned with processes such as speech, balance, seeing, etc., there is a disturbance of normal function in these areas which may correspond to the disturbances experienced during the aura. It has been demonstrated by blood-flow studies that the area of spreading depression moves from the back of the head (occipital lobe) forward over the brain (cortex) at the speed of between 2– 5 mm each minute.

The level of excitability in the brain is controlled by a variety of factors – these include blood sugar levels, oxygen intake, and other chemical factors such as the level of magnesium, which controls levels of inhibition, and potassium, which controls levels of excitation in the brain. Blood levels of the neuro-transmitter, called *serotonin*, fluctuate during migraine (they increase during the pre-headache phase, and drop during the headache). This is likely to be caused by an alteration in blood platelets. Platelets, which store serotonin, exhibit chronic clumping together (aggregation) in migraine sufferers and increase their adhesiveness prior to an attack. They also affect the vasoactive amines in the blood. The vasoactive (acting on blood vessels) amine (a class of substances that can cause inflammation) released into the blood vessels leads to an inflammatory reaction (i.e. painful, distended blood vessels).

A national migraine study of over 20,000 people in the USA showed that 17.6% of women and 5.7% of men experience severe migraine headaches, with the prevalence in lower income groups being more than 60% higher than those with an annual income of more than $30,000. Economic estimates show that the cost of migraine in the United States ranges from $1 billion to $17 billion per year. A survey of almost 15,000 people conducted in 1975 by the British Migraine Trust disclosed that 10% of males and 16% of females suffer from unilateral headache with migrainous characteristics. If bilateral headaches were included, the figures increased to 20% and 26%, respectively. The economic impact of migraine, i.e. the cost to the economy of working days lost through absence due to migraine is huge. The UK's population of 3.7 million migraine sufferers loses 18 million working days each year; six million days' absence and a further 12 million days spent at work, but operating ineffectively because of the debilitating effect of a migraine attack. The financial cost of this disruption has been estimated at nearly £750 million.

Over 1,500 Irish people were surveyed by the Market Research Bureau of Ireland (MRBI) in 1996. Patients aged 15–64 years were interviewed randomly throughout the Republic of Ireland. The results revealed that 8% of the population, or one in every twelve people, suffers regular classic migraine attacks. As a proportion of the

Irish population of 3,523,000, this suggests that over 174,500 people suffer the debilitating effects of true migraine. The survey also revealed that 75% of true migraine sufferers in Ireland are female, a figure borne out by worldwide trends already identified for the illness, with attacks lasting from 4 – 72 hours at a time. The survey found that 26% of all sufferers experience severe migraine attacks more than 20 times per year. Some 11% of sufferers reported losing at least four days per year from work, a potential loss to the economy of 70,000 working days. However, because many sufferers would not seek a medical certificate for one lost day from work during an attack, and others such as the unemployed and women working in the home would not be included, it is difficult to estimate the true cost of migraine-related illness.

Economic cost is only one element. The greatest concern expressed by migraine sufferers was the decrease in the quality of their lives for which no monetary value can be estimated. Although it is not ordinarily life-threatening, a considerable literature expounds the large number of sufferers, the high cost to the person in question and society, and the often crushing effects it has on personal and family life.

Pharmacologic treatment of migraine may be *acute* (abortive, symptomatic) or *preventive* (prophylactic). Patients experiencing frequent severe headache often require both approaches. Symptomatic treatment attempts to abort or reverse a headache once it has started. Preventive therapy is given on a daily basis, even in the absence of a headache, to reduce the frequency and severity of anticipated attacks. Symptomatic treatment is seen as appropriate for most acute attacks. Medications used to treat migraine are: simple analgesics (e.g. paracetamol or soluble aspirin); antiemetics (e.g. maxolon); a combination of the two (e.g. paramax); vasodilators (e.g. ergotamine); anxiolytics; non-steroidal anti-inflammatory drugs; steroids; major tranquillizers; narcotics; and, more recently, selective 5-HT (serotonin) agonists. Preventive treatments include a broad range of medications, most notably beta-blockers, calcium channel blockers, anti-depressants, serotonin antagonists, and anti-convulsants.

Migraine sufferers tend to have a positive family history. Some authors have even considered a positive family history as a prerequisite for the diagnosis of migraine. When only parents and siblings were considered, 46% of migraine sufferers were found to have a family history of migraine, compared to 18% of patients with tension headache used as a control group. When grandparents were included, 55% had a positive family history. By and large, the relative most commonly affected was the mother in 53% of cases; the father in 17%; a sister in 17%; and a brother in 12%. At least one affected relative has been found in 85% of cases.

The era of the molecular genetic analysis of migraine has also begun. A region of DNA on human chromosome 19 was linked to the clinical diagnosis of familial hemiplegic migraine in two large French families. The investigators were able to further localise the critical area to a 30 cM (i.e. a specific length of DNA) region of the genome. The next major scientific achievement will be the identification of the precise gene within this region of DNA that is responsible for the clinical expression of hemiplegic migraine. The factors which may play a part in crossing that migrainous threshold are called *triggers*.

Triggers which have been identified include: environmental factors (altitude change, air pollution, bright sunshine, any flickering light, computer monitors, headbands, tight ponytails, noise, weather changes and odours, e.g. chemicals and perfumes): food (alcohol, dairy produce, caffeine, oils, monosodium glutamate, red wine, chocolate, cheeses, nuts, liver, dried fish, pickled meats, dried fruit, etc.): other triggers include aeroplane trips, hormones, tobacco, dehydration, hypoglycaemia, change in sleep pattern, physical exercise, personality factors and stress. Extremes in the daily biorhythm of sleep, eating, or exercise, and variations in weekday versus weekend habits are common triggers of migraine.

Both too little and too much sleep seem to be headache precipitants. Insufficient sleep has been found to be a trigger for 29% of male and 52% of female medical and dental students. Excessive sleep was cited as a precipitant for 23% of these students' headaches.

Fasting has been found to precede 77% of migraine attacks. Moderately lowered blood sugar produced in a fast is known to cause cranial artery vasodilation, and there are numerous reports of migraine induced by both hypoglycaemia (low blood sugar) and simple fasting.

Exercise can be a double-edged sword in migraine. Moderate exercise has stress-reduction and muscle-relaxation value. Intense effort in exercising beyond one's normal fitness level is capable of triggering a migraine for most migraineurs. During a migraine even mild exercise usually exacerbates pain, probably because of increased blood flow in intercranial arteries. Exercise-induced migraine can be avoided by a 5–10 minute warm-up and a brief cool-down period after the main exercise period. The cool-down activity consists of several minutes of walking, which may be effective by drawing blood from the cranial region to muscles in the lower part of the body which are used for walking.

Extremes of bright light, loud noise, odours, and heat can aggravate or precipitate headache. The percentage of individuals who experience headaches as a result of sensory extremes is as follows: heat (36.7%), noise (29.9%), and light (27.2%). 10%–50% of migraine patients report adverse weather conditions as influencing their attacks.

Stress is also a migraine trigger. Migraine patients report stress as one of the most common headache triggers and the frequency of headache usually increases if the person is worried by some protracted problems. In retrospective studies, 48% of migraine patients and 38% of medical or dental school students observed stress as a migraine trigger. In a prospective study in which migraine patients kept a two-month headache diary, 50% of all migraines were closely related in time to overly-stressful events. The transformation of episodic migraine into severe daily headache may be the result of excessive stress, depression, and/or overuse of analgesic rebound medications. Headache intensity is closely related to poor stress coping skills as well as to stress itself. It has been demonstrated that migraine attacks can be induced by laboratory stress. Daily stress has been demonstrated as an important trigger factor for migraine attacks. In responding to stress, digestion slows down (leading to gastric stasis) so that blood can be sent to the muscles and brain. Heart rate increases, blood pressure rises, breathing becomes faster. Perspiration increases to cool the body and muscles tense. When frequently called into action, the body's response to stress can cause adverse reactions. At times of emergency, migraineurs usually remain free of headache, which then tends to occur as soon as the crises resolves. Similarly, 'weekend headache' occurs at the moment of 'let down' or relaxation after the sustained stress of a working week. An emotional shock may be followed by the symptoms of classic migraine within seconds or minutes.

Few triggers by themselves are sufficiently potent in isolation from other triggers to induce headache all the time or nearly all the time after exposure. Most migraines are precipitated only when several triggers occur in close proximity. Migraine patients report an average of 5.3 triggers per individual, but no study has assessed the mean number of triggers per headache. The summative effect of the triggers occurring together results in the individual's headache threshold being crossed. The headache trigger model has parallels to a current model of heart disease in that a genetic predisposition towards the adverse medical event, i.e. migraine, is potentiated by the additive effect of a number of different possible lifestyle factors such as diet, exercise, stress, etc.

In general, paper and pencil measures of stress and personality find that migraine patients as a group are distinct from non-headache normals, tension headache sufferers, and other pain patients in that they tend to be goal-oriented, exacting and responsible. They may be uneasy with emotions and may focus on getting things done in an orderly manner while denying or ignoring obvious stress or conflict. While the migraine population displays distinct personality traits in comparison with other groups, the differences are not so great as to be applicable to each individual.

Although the pathogenesis of migraine is not clear, available evidence indicates that the majority of migraine attacks are precipitated by strong cognitive and emotional reactivity (whether covert or overt) to increased work pressure, interpersonal problems, difficulties in self-expression, tension and anxiety, ego-threatening situations, and problems involving financial, career, or social position. In other words, there is strong cognitive or emotional reactivity to events perceived as stressful by the migraine sufferer. At present there is no complete 'cure' for migraine. Building up resistance to stress from within can use both psychological and physiological techniques.

(a) Cognitive Appraisal

How a person copes with stress depends upon their cognitive view of the situation. Most migraine patients report that the perception of headache onset is stressful and upsetting; and this stress, in turn, may amplify pain intensity. Patients often react to the first signs of a headache with frustration, anger, or upset as they anticipate increasing migraine discomfort. In addition, a headache may result in inability to function at work, at study or in the home, and in cancelling planned activities. Frequent migraine may be difficult for work associates or family to understand.

(b) Coping with Stress

To handle stress, the person must learn to manage their appraisal of the environment and to manage their stress more effectively. Eliminating stress, *per se*, is not as important as learning to cope with it and to master it. Coping involves both what a person does, thinks and says.

(c) Self-Efficacy

The person must believe that they have the relevant skills and believe they are capable of applying them as needed. This self-efficacy will determine whether they will try to cope with or avoid a situation that they view as beyond their coping ability. Self-efficacy can also determine how much effort a person will invest and how long they will persist in the face of aversive experiences.

(d) Stress Inoculation

Stress inoculation can be described as a type of psychological protection that functions in a similar way to a medical inoculation which provides protection from disease. Stress inoculation gives the person a prospective defence or set of skills to deal with future stressful situations. One of the advantages of stress inoculation is that both relaxation and cognitive coping skills are learned and applied as part of the stress inoculation procedure.

(e) Cognitive Disputation

This model holds that situations and events do not make people disturbed, but it is their beliefs about them that give rise to emotional disturbance. Therefore, cognitive disputation with pain patients would involve helping them to identify their underlying beliefs about pain-related situations.

They include: catastrophising, over-generalising, selective focus, misattribution, all-or-nothing thinking, expecting the worst to happen, making negative prediction, disqualifying the positive, magnification, and minimisation. Identification of problematic thinking, negative self-talk, negative attitudes, guilty thoughts (the tyranny of the 'shoulds') about one's limitations, is the first task patients are required to complete. They would then be coached to utilize cognitive strategies to test the reality of these beliefs and argue against them. Limits are set on self-defeating thoughts and images by learning to abort them before they become overwhelming. The basic technique employed for this purpose is 'thought-stopping', which simply involves interrupting a sequence of negative ideas by vocalising or subvocalising the word 'stop' a number of times and then substituting an alternative flow of thoughts or images. Another technique simply involves noticing when one is having negative thoughts and then reminding oneself to 'let go' of them and refocus positive ideas.

A major goal of therapeutic intervention should be to control or modify emotional reactivity to events perceived as stressful. Migraine patients appear more likely to appraise events as undesirable and stressful, and cope with them in a maladaptive manner. Migraine patients report a significantly greater number of stressful life events than control patients. Although migraine may begin as a genetic/biologic disorder, it quickly becomes entangled with psychosocial factors. Perceived control has been shown and accepted to be a basic mediating variable for both acute and chronic pain. Perceived control has been seen as affecting the patient's perceived self-efficacy of pain regulation. Relaxation training has enabled migraine patients to reduce the frequency and severity of headache. Reviews of numerous studies conclude that learning to relax is an important variable. Relaxation skills are presumed to enable the migraine sufferer to exert control over headache-related physiological responses, and more generally, over sympathetic arousal. Chronic pain patients hyperventilate. Abnormal muscle activity is a factor in many chronic pain syndromes – guarding and grimacing. Relaxation training may also provide a brief hiatus from everyday stresses and assist individuals in achieving a sense of mastery or self-control over symptoms. In addition, changing the individual's cognitive and behavioural responses enhances their ability to control their physiological responses to stressful situations.

Cognitive behavioural therapy focuses on the cognitive and affective components of migraine. The way individuals cope with everyday stress can aggravate or maintain migraine headaches and increase the disability and distress associated with headaches. Cognitive behavioural therapy attempts to help people to identify the kinds of stressful situations that produce their physiological symptoms and to alter the way they cope with these situations. The next step is to identify the expectations or beliefs that might explain the headache reactions. The final step is to change something about the stressful situation, the way of thinking about it or the behaviour. The options might include setting realistic goals that include self-care (morning and afternoon breaks, lunch breaks, adequate rest, exercise and sleep), recognising that the need to perform perfectly leads to unnecessary anguish over errors, or learning to behave more assertively in interactions instead of withdrawing.

Cognitive behavioural interventions are used to teach the person:

1. To identify stressful circumstances that precipitate or aggravate headaches and to employ more effective strategies for coping with these stresses.
2. To cope more effectively with pain and distress associated with headache episodes.
3. To limit negative psychological consequences of recurrent migraine attacks (e.g. depression and disability). Its goal is to help people to cope better with the challenges and stresses of their lives.
4. An approach that has been reviewed is the use of largely home-based, minimal-therapist contact treatments in comparison with traditional, individual, clinic-based treatments. Equivalent levels of headache relief were obtained for limited contact (3 sessions over 8 weeks) versus intensive contact (16 sessions over 8 weeks). The home-based treatments emphasised audiotapes and manuals to guide the home training.

Overall, it seems clear that psychological treatments for headache can be very effectively delivered in a minimal contact format, augmented by an audiotape and written material. Continued practice of what was learned in the formal treatment phases is stressed by most researchers and clinicians. The patients apply their new skills to cope with new exacerbations. Those patients who practise tend to have a better long-term outcome.

Stress and psychosomatic disorders have become more common in modern life, and the need for reducing stress and relaxation has become continually more pressing. Certainly this is so in the self-management of migraine, both with regard to going through an acute attack and, not less, in the prevention of attacks. Most headache sufferers readily acknowledge that it is clearly preferable to prevent headaches or to abort them early on rather than to attempt to ameliorate a headache once it has taken hold; in fact, severe bouts of headache may prove unyielding to even highly potent analgesics.

We may conclude that, overall, there is substantial evidence for the efficacy of a cognitive behavioural approach to migraine headache amelioration (frequency, intensity, duration and degree of incapacitation) when therapy is directed at stress management, relaxation and cognitive coping styles.

Personal Isolation

by

Dr Ann Marie McMahon

There is no doubt that there is a significant relationship between loneliness and stress. However, it is important at the outset to differentiate between 'being alone' and 'being lonely'. For some people, the fantasy of living alone on an island, away from everybody, would be the idea of sheer bliss. They could fantasise about having time to relax, being away from tension, pressures, deadlines, targets, domestic or work-related financial problems. For others, this fantasy would probably be a nightmare. The idea of being stranded on an island on one's own would prove to be a stressful situation, provoking feelings of panic, insecurity and a feeling of being totally alone.

Personal isolation is a very individual concept. Some people can feel very isolated even though they are surrounded by many people and may find themselves lonely in what should be a very enjoyable situation. Very often it is not the actual situation that creates the feeling of isolation. Instead, other underlying issues exist for the person that seem to accentuate themselves when the person is caught in places that exacerbate these feelings.

Take, for example, a woman who has just split up from a long-term relationship. She may find herself at a party for her best friend and notices everybody is in a very elated mood. However, she cannot empathise with this mood as she is aware of how outside the party she feels. For others, when they find themselves in this situation, alcohol may give them the courage to survive the situation. Drink can isolate a person more, because the alcohol can anaesthetise the lonely feelings. If the person becomes dependent on drink, they may end up wanting to drink alone, further isolating themselves from other people – thereby ending up with two problems instead of one.

Others, perhaps those who are going through the experience of the death of a close friend or partner, can feel extremely isolated and the loss is often so traumatic that they become overwhelmed with these feelings. They feel they cannot articulate how they feel. Their loneliness is also related to the fact that people around them do not know what to say or do. They worry that they will not be able to cope without this person in their life and the result is the fear that they will be left alone, never having a close friend or never being able to love somebody else again.

Feelings of loss have nothing to do with age. Just as a little child lost in a shop feels very frightened and alone, a widow or widower in old age can feel the same sense of loss and fear. Loss, loneliness and personal isolation are all very closely interconnected. They result in the fear that nothing will ever change and that they will never be able to enjoy themselves as they did in the past. The loss can often result in low self-esteem and health may even become affected. We become stressed and lose sight of who we are. It is almost as if part of ourselves has been cut off because we feel so alone. This can lead to a loss of confidence and the feeling of total rejection. We feel rejected, not only by the person we have lost, but also we end up rejecting ourselves. We may also feel sad and angry.

When people feel totally isolated and lonely, they end up becoming negative in their outlook and can lose interest in themselves and their appearance. Their negativity can keep them isolated and it can lead to a loss of their sense of humour. They have lost their core and they may end up with no energy left to cope and no support left to call upon.

Different situations can lead to different types of loneliness and personal isolation. For example, the 'empty nest syndrome' can lead parents to feel very lonely for their children. Teachers can feel the same sense of isolation when they retire and are no longer dealing with their pupils on a daily basis. In fact, any sort of retirement can lead to a profound sense of loss. This is because we do not feel connected in some way. We are outside and feel marginalised. Anybody who is feeling marginalised has this feeling of personal isolation. For instance, the woman whose husband is having an affair can feel very isolated because she knows he is not there for her. When she finally discovers he is with somebody else, the feeling is exaggerated again because it confirms her suspicions all along and can justify the feelings she has been having for some time.

People who have feelings of shame or guilt often feel very isolated because they believe the stigma attached to these feelings makes them different to everybody else. The idea of being 'labelled' can also make you feel different and can isolate you from other people. Certain stigmas, like having a label related to mental illness, can make you feel 'outside' because society sometimes doesn't understand what you're going through and is not able to empathise with your situation. Sometimes, a person is so down they feel suicidal.

Others who feel the pain of isolation are those who may have risked being different – nuns who have left their vocation, priests who have left the clergy, or the teenager who has opted out of college. Society often forces us to be the same and if we opt out or are on the outside, society is not there to support us, e.g. members of ethnic minorities, childless couples, the physically disabled, and those suffering illness. While there is the stress of loneliness, there is also the loneliness of stress. People who are in very stressful jobs and have a lot of responsibility can often feel very isolated from their peers. They may wish that they did not have the title of 'chief executive', or 'captain of industry', etc. because it means they are not one of the crowd and cannot enjoy themselves. To be seen 'on top' is paramount, and they feel that they cannot make a mistake. This, in itself, is a stress and they feel isolated from their peers.

Eventually, when stress becomes so severe that you are almost experiencing a burn-out, the personal isolation is very traumatic and can result in ill-health. You may have to take time out and deal with your burn-out. This, in itself, can create feelings of loneliness. You know you have to deal with this on your own and perhaps you are missing the support and buzz that your work normally creates. Time out becomes a lonely journey. Sometimes, those who are constantly surrounded by people in large organisations find being on their own, in any situation, quite traumatic. The buzz masks the need to look at their own inner being, and the idea of setting off on a holiday on their own is a nightmare. They constantly need people around them for approval and to acknowledge their own worth.

The stress of loneliness is different for everyone. The phrase, 'I am lonely' is seldom heard in our society. It is more acceptable to say, 'I have a busy diary, shall I pencil you in', and for this reason lonely people often become further isolated because they are embarrassed to admit they actually feel lonely. There is almost a sense of shame attached to it, a feeling that nobody wants you. Individuals who don't have a partner often turn down invitations because they know it's going to be 'couples only'. We live in a society which is couple-oriented and very often people on their own are left out for this reason.

You will often hear of elderly widows 'dying of a broken heart' because they are unable to cope with being on their own. Being unemployed can create a sense of personal isolation, particularly if you have already been in the workforce. The lack of social contacts can further enhance your isolation. All feelings of personal isolation are unique to each individual and the severity will depend on the crisis in your life.

Sometimes, loneliness can be a form of self-protection. When you are constantly on your own, you cut emotional ties with other people to protect yourself from exposure to hurt, confrontation and even humiliation. The longer you stay on your own, the greater the chance that you will become further isolated and afraid of others. You become passive in your attitude and can end up feeling unwanted, instead of deciding that you can actively contribute to your social situation. Very often the stress of being lonely becomes a vicious circle. Any human contact becomes dissatisfying and you can end up becoming a recluse. In doing so, you cut yourself off from any hope of finding yourself. When we are doing things with other people and enjoying ourselves, we can forget about ourselves. For instance, in stimulating conversation, in sport, or just working together for a common goal we become interested in something other than maintaining our own pretences. As we get to know other people, we feel less of a need to pretend. We eventually become less isolated and the pain of loneliness thaws out.

Sometimes, the stress of loneliness becomes a way of life. When this happens, you often lose the capacity to enjoy life, and no amount of wealth or any success can make up for this feeling. The combination of loneliness and stress can lead to a terrible emptiness where you feel nothing is worthwhile. Emptiness is an indicator that you are not living creatively. It is as if you have no goals and that no goal could be important enough to you. Sometimes, you end up saying, 'Life has no purpose' or 'Life is not worthwhile'. This failure mechanism can become self-perpetuating, and fear prevents you from breaking the vicious cycle.

In the long-term, emptiness can become a way of avoiding responsibility and become an excuse or a justification for feeling the way you are. Emptiness can also be the symptom of an inadequate self-image. An individual may achieve success but derive little or no sense of satisfaction from it. Being unable to take the credit for an accomplishment because of the internal pain of loneliness may leave you feeling undeserving and inferior.

Even individuals who have achieved success can feel guilty, insecure or anxious when they realise they have succeeded. They feel as if they don't deserve it and it is phoney in some way. Striving for phoney success, to please other people, brings phoney satisfaction. The notion of 'pretending' in our society can also be associated with the stress of loneliness. Pretending you are something you are not implies that you are in conflict with yourself and can lead to loneliness. You feel as though you are observing a stranger playing the role of you.

Isolation, instituted as a defence, may become part of your way of life. You become a person who cannot tolerate closeness or intimacy. People like this are afraid of others, afraid to reach out, afraid to give, and afraid of demands. They distance themselves from others in order to avoid the danger of being treated coldly or even being treated with hostility. They develop the habit of staying away, not from everybody, but from people who might hurt them

Very often this detachment is based on a sensitivity to criticism or rejection. Some people are always searching for a magic relationship to heal the emptiness, but when searching for that relationship, they are merely looking for someone who allows them to express themselves without opposition or criticism. This fear of being criticised can also lead them to strive for perfection, and the stress of having everything right and always being in control of their lives can keep others at a distance. They are afraid to make mistakes and often feel uncertain about their own self-worth.

Likewise, we may resent the success and happiness of others because it proves to us that life is short-changing us and we are being treated unfairly. Very often, resentment is our attempt to make our own failure palpable by explaining it in terms of unfair treatment or injustice. Resentment, however, is like a deadly poison to the spirit and makes happiness impossible. It uses up tremendous energy and ensures further alienation from people around us. When people do not warm to us, we carry chips on our shoulders, and find further reasons for being resentful.

However, resentment is not caused by other people, events or circumstances. It is caused by our own reaction to our emotional responses. What you have to understand is that resentment and self-pity are not ways to happiness or success but lead to defeat and cause unhappiness. In fact, resentful people turn over their reins to other people. They give power to another person and are dependent on other people. They make unreasonable demands and claims on others. Resentment is, therefore, inconsistent with creative goal-striving. In order to help you overcome this problem of resentment, which creates a combination of loneliness and stress, you should start striving for goals which are important to you and consistent with your own deep, inner needs.

The stress of loneliness can occur at any time in our lives. However, the combination of early retirement and increased life expectancy means that many people will spend as long in retirement as they did in work. But coping with retirement requires planning. More and more people who have seen their families reared are also moving from bigger family homes into a smaller, more manageable house. A lifetime of memories is left behind, increasing the stress of loneliness.

Compulsory retirement, for some people, leads to stress-related illness because they do not take the time to plan, to adjust, and to be psychologically ready to accept major changes in their lives. Many people do not have a clear idea of how to structure their daily routine. For perhaps twenty-five or thirty years their day has been planned according to a work schedule. Even their leisure time has been planned with their partner and they do not have to think what it is like to face scheduling their day.

Those forced into retirement also have to look at areas that never challenged them before. Vital areas include psychological health, financial stability and also having to make an effort to keep in daily contact with other people. It is also important for the retired person to consider his or her partner, particularly if the other person stayed at home.

When we are faced with the loss of something that made us feel very secure, it leaves us very vulnerable. We feel extremely raw and want to further isolate ourselves so that nobody can see our open

101

wound. As children, adults comfort us from any stress and trauma and we are never left on our own. But we are not prepared when, in adulthood, we have to face this experience. The sudden death of a partner means not alone that we have to go through the whole grief process but that we are not prepared to cope with having to live independently and on our own.

For many, it is the suddenness of being put in a situation that you are not prepared for that creates terrible tensions and stress. Moving into any new situation undoubtedly brings its own fears. There is the danger that we will postpone enjoyment because we hold on to our fears. Fear of the unknown and fear of the future are two of our worst enemies. Even when someone tells us that something will turn out to our advantage, we still won't do it. We feel rooted and paralysed. We may seem stubborn, awkward or even hostile because others don't understand the extent of our fear.

Fear prevents us from changing. It gets us stuck in such a way that we end up becoming our own worst enemies. Even the aged who move into nursing homes have to cope with adjustment at a very late time in life. Again, it is this moving away from the comfort of the family and moving away from friends that creates enormous fears and can turn what may have been a very happy person into a lonely, old and unhappy one.

To avoid creating more stresses than we are experiencing, it is important that we start recognising what is happening to us. Unless we deal with the signals, the pain of loss, the anxiety and the stress will only multiply to such an extent that we lose sight of who we really are. There is also a feeling of being out of control, as if life has dealt a very hard blow and you can't hit back. It is very important that you talk about how you are feeling. Find somebody who will listen to how you are feeling, a family member, a friend, a partner, a neighbour and if you still feel very uncomfortable about sharing your innermost thoughts with a close one, seek profession help. It is important to have somebody to listen to what is going on.

Unfortunately, some will find it easier to stay locked behind those negative doors. Fear of change keeps us immobilised. Some people actually prefer the familiarity of such a negative existence. They may feel afraid of change, so it becomes easier to stay put rather than reach out to sample new territory. Frequently, increased negativity comes about through weighty emotions like guilt or worry. They threaten to anchor us and to keep us shackled. Try to prioritise and understand what you should do initially, rather than feeling that you have to do everything at the one time. Take things slowly. Be kind and gentle to yourself. Recognise the areas of negativity and decide how you are going to cope, one step at a time. You realise you are now moving into something new. Don't be afraid of making mistakes. Listen for any negative thinking and catch it before it can set down roots.

Get support. It is important that you acknowledge your situation, recognise that you can get help and be able to share your situation with another person, be it a friend, self-help group or professional. Learn to deal with the initial loss or feelings of loneliness, rather than multiplying your problems. Recognise that it will take time to get over certain situations but that things can get better. Remember that there is always an answer to your problem.

Stress in the Workplace

by

Gerard Butcher

'I woke up and looked at the alarm clock. My feelings of calm and relaxation turned to horror when I realised that I had overslept by 30 minutes. My stomach flipped over several times when I remembered that my boss was expecting me to make an important presentation to the Japanese delegation first thing this morning. He had reminded me several times that getting this contract was vitally important if our company was to remain viable. 'In other words,' I thought, 'Mess this one up, Jim and you'll be to blame if the company goes under! Thanks a lot, boss.' I'd even switched the phone off all day yesterday to concentrate on completing my presentation. I picked up my rechargeable battery-operated razor and switched it on. Nothing happened. I checked the battery level. Zip! Nothing! I'd forgotten to switch on the recharger last night.

By now, chaos reigned. Everybody wanted to get into the bathroom while I was shaving, using my wife's throwaway razor which she usually used for her legs! It wasn't doing a good job. I left the house without breakfast, leaving my family screaming and shouting for one thing and another. My wife seemed really hurt when I shouted at her and the children to get out of my way. I felt bad about that, but thought I would deal with it later. After all, surely our steady income was important? Having been made redundant last year, I was very fortunate to get a new job within 10 weeks. I hated attending the dole office.

104

Then I hit the traffic. Leaving later than usual meant that the rush-hour traffic had lots of time to build up while I was enjoying my beauty sleep. I couldn't believe the length of the queue from our estate just to get onto the main road. There was nothing I could do but sit and wait, fuming. It was only then I noticed the small trickle of blood on my shirt from a cut on my neck. I rubbed it in panic which only made it worse. Again, nothing I could do. By now, all I could think of was my boss sitting waiting in his office with the Japanese delegation, smiling at them and putting on a brave face while wondering where I was. My heart was pounding, I felt sweat trickle down my face and underarms. My stomach felt sick. Waves of panic came over me every few minutes as I thought of all the excuses I could make, none of which sounded convincing. I thought that maybe I would do the honourable Japanese thing and commit ritual Hari-Kari by announcing my resignation publicly and save my company's honour.

Eventually, I arrived at the office an hour behind schedule. At this stage, I was so filled with gloom and foreboding that I just casually walked into the building. I could see my boss standing inside the door waiting to greet me. Strangely, he seemed remarkably calm. I supposed he'd had a lot of time to think about my sacking and how he would go about it. He could be quite ruthless when he chose to be. 'Jim,' he said, 'Where were you? I've been trying to get you on the phone since early yesterday evening, but it seemed to be out of order. The Japanese aren't coming until tomorrow. They were flying via the US for some other business deal and got delayed by storms. We've rescheduled the meeting for Wednesday. Why not take today off and relax before your presentation ...?'

In some way or other most of us can identify with Jim. Stress is a common experience. Because companies are primarily in the business of making money, many employees feel the stress imposed on them by mergers, takeovers, currency fluctuations, privatisation, etc. We experience increased workloads, longer working hours and more accountability. Because of the rapid advancement in technology, our skills must be constantly updated. 'Flexibility' has become a buzzword for many. Increasingly, it appears that things are going to stay like this for the future. What do you think when you see middle and senior managers being replaced by younger, fitter, and more zealous underlings? Does it mean more opportunity for you, or do you realise that some day, maybe sooner than you thought, you'll be called into the manager's office, not for a chat about promotion, but rather to find him struggling to tell you in a nice way that you're not needed anymore? It's strange, but unemployed people are often told that they don't have enough work experience to be employed. Of course, unless a company chooses to employ them they will remain inexperienced, and unemployed. At the other end of the scale, we now have employees being told that their experience doesn't count. Younger people can be brought onboard more cheaply. So, how do you cope in all of this? How do you hold on, not just to your job, but to your sanity? How do you prevent yourself from becoming a victim of work-related stress? My hope is that, in this chapter, I can help to answer some of these questions under the following headings:

1. What is workplace stress?
2. What are the effects of stress in the workplace?
3. Is work always the problem?
4. How can you identify how much stress is bad for you?
5. How can you learn to deal with stress in your workplace?

To begin, it is important to understand what we mean by stress. After all, many people in our society today talk about stress. Nearly everyone has their own understanding of it, and there are many definitions. One which I particularly favour is given by the European Foundation for the Improvement of Living and Working Conditions, an EU-funded body based in Dublin. In one of their recent reports they suggest that stress can be defined as follows:

> *'A stress is any force that puts a psychological or physical factor beyond its range of stability, producing a strain within the individual. Knowledge that a stress is likely to occur constitutes a threat to the individual. A threat can cause a strain because of what it signifies to the person.'*

That last bit about what stress signifies to the person is important and I shall return to it later in the section on how to deal with stress. How, though, can we define stress in the working environment? Again, we can turn to the European Foundation for the Improvement of Living and Working Conditions. They define workplace stress as follows:

'Job stress refers to a situation wherein job-related factors interact with a worker to change (i.e. disrupt or enhance) his or her psychological and/or physiological conditions such that the person (i.e. mind or body) is forced to deviate from normal functioning.'

In other words, what used to work doesn't work anymore. That, sociologists tell us, places an individual in a crisis which can only be resolved by finding a new way forward. Failure to do so leaves the individual in a state of crisis, i.e., under stress. If this state of crisis continues over a period of time, and more importantly, if an individual then begins to believe that no matter what they do the situation remains the same, feelings of helplessness start to creep in. These feelings of helplessness can be the precursors of depression and anxiety attacks.

The effects of stress, in themselves, are many and varied. Aside from the sheer unpleasantness of the feeling of being stressed, research in this area has implicated stress in the incidence and development of:

- Coronary heart disease.
- Mental illness.
- Certain types of cancer.
- Poor health behaviours such as smoking, dietary problems, lack of exercise, excessive alcohol consumption and drug abuse.
- Life and job dissatisfaction.
- Accidents and careless or unsafe behaviours at work.
- Marital and family problems.
- A whole range of more minor physical and psychological conditions including migraine, stomach ulcers, hay fever, skin rashes, impotence, menstrual problems, insomnia, panic attacks, irritability, poor concentration, anxiety and indecisiveness.

I'm sure you'll agree that this is quite a sizeable list. However, stress in the workplace carries its own particular burdens, both for the workforce in general and for companies. Consider this list of concerns about workplace stress voiced by the United Kingdom's Principal Medical Officer at the Department of Health, Dr R. Jenkins:

- Reduced productivity, ineffective working, missing deadlines, making faulty assessments and decisions.
- Labour turnover: sufferers from anxiety and depression are more likely to leave their jobs of their own accord; thus recruitment and retraining of their replacements may be costly.
- Poor timekeeping, poor interpersonal relationships with colleagues, superiors, inferiors and clients.
- Accidents: stress is considered to be responsible for between 60–80% of all workplace accidents.

Quite aside from the effects of absences because of stress, being stressed in work obviously has a huge impact as evidenced by the above list. Consider too, that it is reckoned that, for every single day lost to an industrial dispute, 30 working days are lost to depression and anxiety. I'm sure you'll agree that in reading down through this list it becomes imperative that, as a society, we need to understand more about stress in the workplace. More importantly, we need to consider how to deal with it effectively.

Inasmuch as we need to identify factors in the workplace which cause stress, it is also important to remember that some issues outside of work which are stressful can be brought into our working environments. It is helpful if we do not blame the wrong issue as the cause of our stress. Not too long ago, an individual came to see me complaining of work-related stress. He was a senior manager in a company where the workforce were expected to meet a variety of deadlines, all seemingly equally important. In his position, he felt pushed at one end by more senior personnel in the company to produce results from his underlings. It was also made clear to him that failure to produce results would be seen as a personal failure. As a result, this gentleman felt compelled to proofread all reports before sending them up the line to ensure that they were accurate. From the other end, his team complained of the pressure which they felt under to complete their various reports, and also felt that their work was being undermined by his constant checking. Result? Understandable stress. However, a more detailed assessment showed that there were considerable marital stresses, not all of which could be attributed to the demands of work, although the work factors were being blamed. In this instance, it was soon obvious that factors both inside and outside work were causing stress. A solution in this instance came partially through the channel of an assertiveness training programme. As a result of teaching him appropriate assertion techniques, he found that he was able to identify and prioritise his own needs, and then more ably deal with demands within his workplace and at home.

With regard to the working environment itself, many factors have been identified which have their place in causing stress to arise. These include:

1. Lack of job discretion, i.e. not being involved in decisions which affect you.
2. Low use of your job skills.
3. Too few or too many work demands.
4. Low task variety.
5. High degrees of uncertainty or insecurity about work permanence.
6. Poor pay or lack of recognition for work.
7. Unpleasant physical working conditions.
8. Low interpersonal support from colleagues or superiors, including being exposed to issues of prejudice or harassment.

If any, or indeed more than just one, of the items on this list apply to you, it would not be surprising if you felt under stress. Should it be the case that you are unsure of being able to discriminate between work and other factors which may be the source of your stress, it might be a good idea to keep a journal for a couple of weeks. In this journal keep a daily record of your emotional state, perhaps every two hours. Each time you make an entry take note of what you have been doing or thinking about at the time. Over a period of time, patterns or sources of stress should emerge. Having completed this task it is important to be able to identify how much stress you are suffering and then to determine what can be done to deal with it effectively.

Being able to identify when or if your stress levels are at a danger point can be important for several reasons. If you are aware, then it means that you can do something about it. Conversely, if you remain unaware of stress levels rising and staying high for a prolonged period of time, the consequences may be more serious and subsequent treatment may take longer. You may, under these circumstances, also require additional time off work to recover. Early recognition then, may save you considerable upset later on. The Health Education Council in the United Kingdom have produced a self-completing Stress Rating Questionnaire which is reproduced below. You may, if you wish, fill it out. It may also be a good idea to give the questionnaire to someone else close to you to fill in on your behalf. This may give you a view of yourself which could prove worthwhile.

Stress Rating Questionnaire.

Answer the following questions in terms of the past 12 months. If your answer is *yes*, tick the box on the right. A score is given for each answer.

1. Have you lived or worked in a noisy area? ☐ 3
2. Have you changed your living conditions or moved? ☐ 3
3. Have you had trouble with your in-laws? ☐ 3
4. Have you taken out a large loan or mortgage? ☐ 3
5. Have you tended to fall behind with the things you should do? ☐ 3
6. Have you found it difficult to concentrate at times? ☐ 3
7. Have you frequently had trouble going to sleep? ☐ 3
8. Have you found that you tend to eat, drink or smoke more than you really should? ☐ 3
9. Have you watched three or more hours of television daily for weeks at a time? ☐ 3
10. Have you or your spouse changed jobs or work responsibilities? ☐ 4
11. Have you been dissatisfied or unhappy with your work or felt excessive work responsibility? ☐ 4
12. Has a close friend died? ☐ 4
13. Have you been dissatisfied with your sex life? ☐ 4
14. Have you been pregnant? ☐ 4
15. Have you had an addition to the family? ☐ 4

16. Have you worried about making ends meet? ☐ 4
17. Has one of the family had bad health? ☐ 4
18. Have you taken tranquillizers from time to time? ☐ 4
19. Have you frequently found yourself becoming easily irritated when things don't go well? ☐ 4
20. Have you often experienced bungled human relations even with those you love most? ☐ 4
21. Have you found that you're often impatient or edgy with your children or other family members? ☐ 4
22. Have you tended to feel restless or nervous a lot of the time? ☐ 4
23. Have you had frequent headaches or digestive upsets? ☐ 4
24. Have you experienced anxiety or worry for days at a time? ☐ 5
25. Have you often been so preoccupied that you have forgotten where you have put things (such as keys) or forgotten whether you've turned off appliances on leaving home or office? ☐ 5
26. Have you been married or reconciled with your spouse? ☐ 5
27. Have you had a serious accident, illness or surgery? ☐ 5
28. Has anyone in your immediate family died? ☐ 6
29. Have you divorced or separated? ☐ 7

Fill in your total points for *yes* answers.

Ratings for stress questionnaire:

- *0–10 points:*

    You're in great shape! Congratulations.

- *11–20 points:*

    You obviously have some stress, but seem to be handling it well enough. Watch out for increases in stressful situations.

- *21–35 points:*

    You are entering the danger zone. You should try and take the pressure off yourself.

- *36–50 points:*

    You are under an excessive amount of stress. See your doctor for a check-up and avoid taking on additional pressures.

Dealing with stress in the workplace can be carried out at both the corporate and personal level. From the perspective of the corporation, a variety of in-house services may be helpful. The bottom line here is that spending a comparatively small amount of money on stress prevention may save a lot more money later on. The European Foundation for the Improvement of Living and Working Conditions suggest the following:

- Provision of on-site fitness and relaxation/exercise classes.
- Corporate membership or concessionary rates at local health and fitness clubs.
- Smoking cessation programmes.
- Introduction of cardiovascular fitness programmes.
- Advice on alcohol and dietary control.
- Design of 'healthy' canteen meals.
- Regular health checks and health screening.
- Stress education and advice on lifestyle management.
- Provision of psychological counselling.

Many people may remember the strike-torn times that characterised the motor manufacturing industry in the United Kingdom in the 1970s. Aside from trying to deal with the trade unions, some of these companies, including Ford, Rover and Lucas, attempted to encourage the desire to learn which they found among their employees. In Britain, the National Commission on Education reported on how these companies ran schemes which encouraged their employees to learn new skills which, interestingly, did not have to be job-related. Some, for example, decided that they would like to learn a foreign language for holidays. Many others decided to take vocational courses in engineering or word-processing. The common experience was that these schemes were successful and had many benefits, including not only a rise in self-esteem and confidence in the employees who participated, but as a result those concerned became more interested in job-related training opportunities which the company had to offer. Opportunities for stress to take a hold in this sort of environment must be considerably reduced. Perhaps there is a lesson for many companies here.

On an individual level there are numerous steps which can be taken. Apart from general considerations of moderation in diet, alcohol, exercise, etc., I would like to cover these steps more particularly under the headings of lifestyle, 'parking' your problems, and your personal cognitive style.

The first step here is to identify precisely how you would like your life to be different. Within this context, it may be useful to consider all aspects of your day-to-day living. The aim is to attempt to achieve some degree of balance between work, home and leisure activities. Begin by writing down how many hours you devote each week to these three areas of your life. Remember to note how often you take work home (Incidentally, most people who take their briefcases home to do extra work never even open them. Result? Unnecessary guilt!) You might also check to see if you take your full annual leave entitlement. Now decide how much time you can reasonably give to bring about change in those areas. Try not to be too ambitious as you may only be setting yourself up for failure. Now to the tricky bit! Many people trying to work out ways of reducing their stress levels have a general idea of what they would wish to change in their lives, but fall down on the specifics. For example, you might make a note to generally take more time away from the working environment and say to yourself, 'I must play more golf.' Six months later, with a variety of deadlines and other pressures, that idea may have been consigned to the dustbin of good, but impractical, thoughts. The idea would probably work better by taking out your diary, making a list of specific times over the next year when you will take that time off for your game of golf. Better still, call up your golfing partners and get them to do the same. This way, if someone calls to make an arrangement, that particular space in your diary is already filled. Right now why not make a specific note of changes which you would like to make in your lifestyle over the next twelve months? Write them down in the column below:

1...
2...
3...
4...

Having completed this task, take out your diary and mark out particular times when you will carry out these changes to your lifestyle. These might include going swimming, taking your son to a football match, going away with your partner for a weekend or simply taking a daily 20-minute brisk walk at lunchtime, three times a week. Again, I must stress the need to be as specific as possible in order to increase the chances of success.

The next step in stress management may be to learn how to 'park' problems on a regular basis. One technique which has been found to be of benefit to those of an obsessional nature is to practise 'postponing' their worries until a later time. In other words, if an issue is bothering you or causing you some concern, agree with yourself to worry about it or deal with it at a specified time later in the day or the following day. It may seem very simple, but it does actually work. In this instance, if you are concerned about a meeting which is due to take place next week, and in the meantime you have a deadline to meet regarding another matter, make a note in your diary to sort out your concerns about the meeting at a specified time. Giving yourself this kind of distance from a problem may help to change your perspective. When the time comes round to dealing with the problem you have 'postponed', you may well find that it doesn't really require that much attention, or your approach will be fresher having distanced yourself from it over a short period of time.

Among the many reasons why stress may affect some more than others is the way they process situations mentally. The old adage – 'Two men looked out from the window of a prison cell: one saw stars, the other saw bars' applies here. How you view your circumstances may well determine how stressed you become. In 1988, ABB, a multinational Swedish company, as part of a review of the company overall, found that only one out of every four of their engineering workers viewed the company in a positive light. Many of the managers found the negative attitudes depressing. Some of the managers, though, took a different attitude. Their view was that if the company could be successful (which it was) under these circumstances, then if they could improve on these attitudes among the workforce, they had the potential to become world-beaters. This particular management attitude has a lesson for us all. If you choose to view your circumstances only in a negative light, you then limit what you can do about your situation.

A friend of mine told me recently of an incident where she had been discussing her work situation with a colleague. Almost everything she had to say was negative. Her colleague sat there listening quietly and then smiled. When challenged about this, her colleague said, 'You're systematically ignoring everything about your job which is good'. Her colleague then went on to list a whole host of circumstances regarding her work situation which my friend had 'forgotten'. This effectively balanced my friend's one-sided view and helped her to view her situation more realistically. My suggestion here is that you make a note of your attitudes towards your work and your colleagues. Now draw up a balance sheet, thus giving thought to both sides of the equation. If you are leaning almost entirely toward the negative, discussing the situation with other colleagues or friends may help. Be careful about how you do this. Sometimes, when we think negatively about a work situation we have a tendency to cultivate work-related friendships among those who will agree with our own point of view. Make sure that you also include someone who may not always see things your way. You can ask yourself if there are other ways of viewing your work? Are there aspects of work which bring some enjoyment or satisfaction to you? How could these be enhanced? Are you holding on to the view that nothing is going to change, so why bother anyway'? If so, then doing nothing about your own attitude means nothing will change. Giving yourself alternative ways of viewing your situation means that you give yourself choices in how you can respond. Knowing you have a choice can be helpful, in itself, in reducing stress.

In this chapter, I have attempted to explore issues around stress in the workplace and what can be done to deal with it. The final point for consideration is that the responsibility for doing something about the stress which you are experiencing rests squarely on your own shoulders. Don't fall into the trap of thinking that everything will be okay when you take your holiday (though that may be a consideration) or when your boss decides to retire, or the next project is completed. You can do something about stress, you do not have to simply suffer it. For your own sake, the sake of your family, and possibly your company, do it now rather than wait to be told by a doctor after an admission to hospital for that stress-related heart attack that you need to examine your lifestyle!

12

Child Sexual Abuse

by

Dr Miriam Moore

Our normal, biological response to danger is to fight and defend or to run away. However, if we are confronted with the possibility of an overwhelming, life-threatening event over which we feel we have no control, our normal *'fight or flight'* response no longer functions and we are rendered totally powerless.

In the aftermath of such an experience, with its attendant feelings of personal devastation and powerlessness, some people can develop *Post-Traumatic Stress Disorder* (PTSD). Indeed, anyone of us can be cast into the dark, nightmarish state of the disorder if we are exposed to an atrocity which is of sufficient magnitude and outside the range of what we perceive to be normal human experience.

The symptoms of PTSD are a function of our human attempts to struggle with events that cannot be experienced, processed and mastered in an adaptive manner using the usual mode of coping. PTSD symptoms can also result from the cumulative effects of severe ongoing stress such as that experienced by victims of incest, children of alcoholics and soldiers in certain war situations. War and rape have been described as the public and private forms of organised social violence. Both are experienced mostly by people in their early adult life. The evidence shows that it is young people who are most likely to develop PTSD.

The developing brain is especially impressionable and sensitive to stress, and because of this children are the most vulnerable of all to developing PTSD in the wake of traumatic experiences. Judging from the numbers of women who are now seeking help because of sexual abuse in childhood and also from the huge numbers of calls on *Childline*, it would seem that there are currently all too many helpless children all over Ireland who are subjected to the prolonged and severe stress of incest. Many of these children will develop PTSD and will be left with deep psychological wounds that do not heal but continue to fester and pour forth their poison way beyond childhood. The trauma of incest etches indelible imprints on the psyche. Profound changes occur in the function of a child's nervous system which can alter the hormonal balance and suppress the immune system. Thus, the foundations are laid for a bleak future overshadowed by a host of physical and psychiatric problems. The psychological and biological damage done to child victims of incest is tenacious and tends to deteriorate rather than improve with the passage of time.

People who were exposed to the trauma of prolonged captivity, such as hostages, prisoners of war and concentration camp survivors, were found to be suffering from full-blown PTSD 35-40 years after their release. It is not surprising, therefore, to find that adult survivors of childhood incest, which is also a form of captivity and torture, also suffer from the disorder in varying degrees of intensity ranging from mild, low-grade to severe psychotic-like symptoms.

PTSD is a peculiar disorder in so far as it may not emerge immediately after trauma and can remain latent only to strike months, years or even decades later. During the latency period, however, there are usually many indications that all is not well. There may be sleep problems, a constricted lifestyle or a general sense that one is just going through the motions of living with little capacity for joy or deep feeling. During the latency period, the symptoms of PTSD can suddenly appear if the victim is exposed to another emotionally disturbing event. The event may be something as major as a death, or a car accident or something which, on the surface, seems relatively minor but is in some way a symbolic reminder of the sexual abuse.

Adult survivors of incest who develop PTSD struggle night and day with nameless anxieties and demented, unresolved feelings for which there seems to be no release. They struggle with fear over loss of control over their own mood swings; with shame and rage over what happened and sadness over their lost childhood and innocence. The majority suffer protracted sorrow and depression, sometimes of suicidal proportion. Adult survivors are also vulnerable to a whole spectrum of somatic problems, including anorexia, bulimia, asthma, allergies, tension headaches, gastrointestinal disturbances and pains in the abdominal, back or pelvic regions.

Alcohol or other drugs are often resorted to in an attempt to obtain some rest and escape from relentless tension and mental misery. These problems usually coexist with and mask PTSD and the original trauma.

Many adult incest survivors tend to suffer from a most insidious and progressive form of PTSD called *complex PTSD*. In addition to the usual morbid symptoms of *ordinary PTSD* including uncontrollable mood swings, fragmented memories, apprehension, hyper-alertness, phobias and sleep disturbances, victims of complex PTSD can also suffer from dissociative states such as chronic amnesia, denial, hallucinations, somnambulism, and in rare cases, multiple personality disorder.

Incest also puts adult survivors at greater risk of repeated victimisation in adult life; they are more likely to be bullied and mistreated. Some studies show that approximately two-thirds of women who have been incestuously abused in childhood are subsequently raped. It seems as though their childhood experiences of fear and learned helplessness undermine their capacity to assert or defend themselves from the onslaughts of aggressors. Child incest and exploitation have always been endemic to patriarchal families; but because of the power of domestic dictators and the conditioned subordination and dependence of their women, their hideous secrets could remain hidden and secure behind doors of polished respectability and normality.

Indeed, maintaining an outward appearance of respectability and normality seems to be the name of the game for the incestuous relatives. And it is this very normality and respectability which is so disturbing. There are no visible signs of perversion or sadism by which incestuous men may be identified. On the contrary, many of the offenders are conventional, respected and hard-working members of the community; they may even appear to be charming, altruistic or sympathetic. Moreover, they usually present a strictly religious and moralistic front to the world at large. In many ways, they are the masters of camouflage and hypocrisy; the proverbial street angels and house devils. In stark contrast to his congenial public demeanour, the incestuous father tends to rule his household with the iron hand of a pompous and tyrannical despot.

Money is often used as a means of control and is doled out in measured amounts in return for gratitude and servility. He may further attempt to disempower family members through emotional isolation. Attitudes to outsiders tend to be hostile, critical and border on the paranoid. Friendships, especially those with the opposite sex, are positively discouraged.

The sexual abuser is, in actual fact, an addict. The child is his drug and he cannot do without his fix. The abusive father/brother tends to perform his deeds in secrecy, often in darkened rooms and in a ritualistic fashion. Silence tends to prevail, except perhaps for stereotyped commands and directions. Seldom is there any eye contact and there is usually a pretence that what is happening is not actually happening. Afterwards, everything has to appear normal as though the sexual abuse has never occurred. The child has no choice but to comply because of her helplessness and dependency. Under the guise of pseudo-normality, she exists in a constant state of tension, never knowing when the next invasion of her little body and soul will take place. The wounded child is forced to bear the crushing burden of her terrible secret as she struggles through her lost childhood.

Abusers secure the compliance of their victim through the use of fear and threats. Sometimes, they use bribes, declarations of love or tell the child that she is the favourite or is special. But deep in her heart, the child knows that she is being wronged and her trust betrayed by the very person who should be her protector.

More often than not, the mother of the abused child is traditional, subservient and often lives in fear of provoking the disapproval of her lord and master. She and her children are, in many ways, comparable to slaves in domestic captivity. Some mothers genuinely do not know about the sexual abuse; others do, but because of their own needs, weaknesses, fears and dependency, they feign ignorance and silently surrender their daughter.

Because the desperate truth of the abused child's life is never openly acknowledged or validated, all conversations with her mother are contaminated with a sense of unreality and infectious irrelevance. Current investigation of PTSD shows that a traumatic event in itself, is not always sufficient to account for the development of PTSD. The disorder develops in the aftermath of trauma; it does not occur right away.

The child who is sexually interfered with is in grave danger of developing PTSD when she is condemned to secrecy and silence.

However, there is less risk of permanent, emotional damage if there is someone there at the time to help, comfort and validate her feelings. Timely and appropriate support and validation from the mother in the wake of the child's traumatic experience can make all the difference in restoring her endangered equilibrium and thus help prevent the symptoms of PTSD from occurring or at least mitigate their severity if they do occur. The lack of protection and sense of abandonment and betrayal by the mother tends to cause the child the deepest of sorrows and can leave her with an abnormal lifelong craving for female nurturance and mothering.

When they reach adulthood, some PTSD/incest victims still remain prisoners of their past, and embark on different life paths. Some become prostitutes, alcoholics, drug addicts or psychiatric patients or dropouts. Many lead lives that are ostensibly 'normal' and may be very successful in their chosen careers and many get married. A woman with a legacy of incest and PTSD, brings to marriage a gruesome emotional dowry.

There are at least six areas in interpersonal relationships in which PTSD/ incest victims are likely to have problems:

1. Getting on with people.
2. Getting emotionally close to someone.
3. Family problems.
4. Inability to express feelings to those they care about.
5. Marital problems.
6. Sexual difficulties.

Unlike a person who has a physical injury or disability, it is not possible to recognise someone who is suffering from PTSD and who is suffering from these problems. Inner tensions and torment can be hidden and the outer personality which is presented to the world may be quite pleasing, particularly on a short-term basis. However, living with a PTSD/incest victim on a day-to-day basis and trying to have a close relationship with them can be quite difficult, depending on the severity of the symptoms.

It is not easy living with a woman who often seems remote, irritable, yells at the children and flies into irrational rages. A woman whose sense of self-worth is debased; her body image sullied; her basic trust in a relationship rent asunder; a woman who feels different and disconnected from others; her mind burning in a dark inferno of nameless anxieties; a woman who is haunted night and day by demonic emotions of rage, shame, sadness and a sense of loss. She may have no understanding as to the source of her inner turmoil and unrest. Chronic amnesia and dissociation, more likely than not, will have eclipsed the unbearable memories of incestuous violation and betrayal.

Sexual intimacy can begin to evoke fragmented memories and flashbacks to primordial scenes of humiliation, terror and revulsion. Sex, at best, is tolerated; she must always feel in control; she is unable to relax and is continuously on guard. Unexpected, affectionate gestures or bodily contact can induce frantic reactions of resistance and outrage. The bewildered husband slowly begins to abandon his dreams of sexual play and harmony. He feels hurt and devastated by his wife's apparent personal rejection and sexual frigidity. The tragedy is that in addition to having stolen her childhood, the rapacious man has also cheated the child of her human birthright – the capacity to surrender joyfully to the abandoned passions of sexual union and ecstasy with her partner.

Eventually, unless help is forthcoming, the husband is forced to bury his dreams of sexual fulfilment and marital harmony in deep hurt and disappointment. The relationship may begin to buckle and disintegrate under the weight of accumulating stresses and difficulties.

The children also become emotionally at risk from living in the tension-ridden environment. As a mother, the incest victim tends to fluctuate between over-protectiveness, withdrawal and outbursts of anger. The children are likely to manifest symptoms of PTSD, including sleep difficulties, nightmares, apathy, sadness, hyperactivity, disruptive behaviour, anxieties or continuous illnesses.

Fortunately, the downward spiral may be stopped with appropriate help and psychotherapy. The vast majority of adult incest survivors, however, do not get help. Instead, they remain silent. Moreover, they keep silent because they are ashamed. Strangely, in the case of incest it is the abused and not the abuser who suffers the life-long pains of stigma and shame. Incestuous men thrive on the silence, shame and isolation of adult survivors. And thus, offenders and potential offenders perpetrate their acts on children without fear and without reprisal. Incest and the enduring, traumatic effects it has on women has, until relatively recently, been shrouded in thick veils of denial and secrecy.

Earlier this century, for example, Freud himself contributed to this denial and secrecy. He was treating women suffering from what he termed *Hysteria*. He discovered during the course of therapy that their hysterical symptoms were due to sexual abuse as children. These symptoms are what we now recognise as PTSD. It is interesting to note that around the same time, thousands of soldiers were returning from World War One suffering from similar symptoms to those of the hysterical women. It could not, of course, be said that men were hysterics; instead, their symptoms were referred to as 'shell-shock' or 'battle fatigue'.

When Freud presented his new findings on hysteria and child sexual abuse to his Victorian colleagues, he was met with stony silence and disapproval. The truth was obviously too uncomfortable for these scientific patriarchs. Freud realised that if he insisted on the truth of his discoveries he would be rejected and his career put in jeopardy. He very quickly, therefore, retracted his original statements and, instead, maintained that the stories of childhood sexual abuse and incest were merely the inventions and false memories of disturbed and hysterical women. Freud finally invented the theory of the Electra and Oedipus Complex whereby children are said to sexually desire their parents. This, of course, has been much more acceptable to society than the tragic reality that it is, in fact, the parent who desires the child! And so Freud's self-interest, his deception and his betrayal of sexually-abused children and women served to maintain the secrecy and ignorance surrounding PTSD and incest for many decades to come.

When PTSD/incest victims do seek help, it is usually on account of associated emotional and physical problems. Unfortunately, therefore, the link between these current problems, such as depression, alcoholism, psychosomatic illnesses, etc. and the original trauma, is unrecognised and the PTSD remains untreated. Until relatively recently, there was little training in the diagnosis and treatment of PTSD for mental health professionals. Because of the prevailing ignorance surrounding the subject, PTSD victims were often misdiagnosed and mistreated, and thus countless numbers of incest women were launched on a lifetime career of psychic pain and frustration. Sometimes, especially in severe cases, the symptoms of PTSD were confused with those of psychosis. Subsequently, many women have ended up in the back wards of mental institutions, alone and abandoned, whilst their abusers roamed free. In the treatment of PTSD per se, whilst short-term treatment with certain antidepressants can be fairly helpful in some cases, pharmaceutical intervention alone, however, is generally ineffective and may even be injurious by serving to repress blocked feelings and so maintain symptoms. Women who are suffering from PTSD as a result of childhood sexual abuse need psychotherapy. Electro-shock therapy should never be resorted to; drugs should only be used when absolutely necessary and as an adjunct to psychotherapy, never as an alternative.

Recovery from psychological trauma can take place only within the context of relationship and psychotherapeutic support; it cannot occur in isolation. Loving support and care are the most important elements in helping women work through the despair and helplessness of incest and PTSD. Psychotherapy demands commitment and courage in order to unearth horrible memories; to work through the unbearable feelings of impacted grief, guilt and rage; to reconstruct a sense of self-worth; to restore trust in life and relationships and ultimately, to find meaning in it all.

It also takes courage to overcome fear and finally confront the abuser. More likely than not, he will deny everything or minimise his crime; the mother and other members of the family may escape into the 'blame the victim' syndrome. They may close ranks with the perpetrator, and the abused may be scapegoated and blamed for causing them trouble and distress. The man who can give love and support to his partner on her journey towards recovery is invaluable. However, in order to do so, he also may need professional help and guidance.

There is no obstacle that the human spirit cannot get over or around when it is truly committed. With love and therapy, the abused adult can eventually transcend the incest trauma so that it no longer darkens the whole of her life or identifies her as a victim. Within herself she can find new strength and depths of feeling born out of pain, learning and courage. It is estimated that 15–20% of those who work through the trauma of incest, go on to become remarkable women and make valuable contributions to society.

Working through the problems surrounding PTSD and incest

enables women to gain a deeper understanding of themselves and of life and to make profound and positive changes in their lives.

Silence, shame and isolation render abused women powerless. But when they unite together and speak out in one voice, they can be unstoppable; together they can hold their heads up high; together they can put the blame and the shame where it belongs; together they can protest and demand validation, restitution and apology for the terrible wrong that has been done to them. The more often women speak out, the more they seek help and the more aware they become, the better they can protect children from the trauma of sexual abuse and the appalling human suffering caused by PTSD.

13

Coping with Schizophrenia

by

Shane Hill

Schizophrenia is the major illness of our time and its sufferers occupy more hospital beds than any other patients suffering with either physical or other psychiatric complaints. It is no respecter of class, colour, creed or intellectual ability and usually strikes between the ages of 16–25 years. It affects nearly 1% of the population on a worldwide basis. There are nearly 40,000 people in Ireland who have a diagnosis of Schizophrenia.

Despite the extensive nature of the illness it is completely misunderstood. A high stress factor for families who have a member diagnosed with Schizophrenia is the stigma, myths, misinformation and widespread ignorance they become aware of, on first hearing the diagnosis. Families tend to have two very different reactions to the word Schizophrenia; those who feel relief that the baffling behaviour of their relative can actually be named, and those who feel insulted or frightened by the name.

However, before a diagnosis of Schizophrenia is made families will invariably have been trying to understand and cope with bizarre behaviour, noticing that their loved one is expressing strange thoughts or unusual feelings which gradually worsen over time. They may even have been enduring aggressive outbursts from their relative. Unlike with a physical illness, there is nothing the family can see or even relate to, which indicates to them the most effective course of action to take.

As the sufferer is losing the control of his mind under a sea of terrifying thoughts and becoming more isolated from his family and society in general, the families are at a complete loss as to how to understand or explain what is happening. This can lead to a breakdown in communication and to families being tempted to blame their relative for causing such a crisis. When the family begin to realise what is the cause of the disruption at home, they need reassurance and information; they need to know that they did not cause the illness but they may still feel guilty because of the genetic nature of it. They may be unrealistic in their hopes for the future and need help and time to grieve for the past dreams they held for their relative's future. They may also need assistance to adopt more realistic expectations for the very different person who is now their relative. Families may feel guilty that they did not realise that their sufferer was 'ill' at an earlier stage and, therefore, did not look for professional help sooner. However, with an illness as complex as Schizophrenia, families have to appreciate that there is no way they could have been able to distinguish the illness from adolescent moodiness and normal personality changes at onset. Usually, after the first episode of Schizophrenia, the situation eventually gets out of control and the GP is called in. If this is during a crisis the sufferer may be hospitalised immediately or may require a visit to a psychiatrist at an out-patient clinic.

It is exceedingly difficult for relatives to accept that despite the fact that Schizophrenia does not affect the intellectual ability of the sufferer, it does affect their ability to cope with any kind of stress, even stress caused by basic life events. A high source of stress for families is that having a relative diagnosed with Schizophrenia is not a community-recognized loss and therefore there are no rituals in society to help them come to terms with it.

Once the sufferer is admitted to hospital, the world remains an extremely frightening place, for both the sufferer and the family. The first time someone goes into a psychiatric ward, they confront head-on all the negative images from their own experiences. Stigma still surrounds most mental illnesses, particularly Schizophrenia. A family's sense of guilt at having put their son or daughter in hospital is often enormous. If there are younger siblings, the emotional drain of a hospital visit can become a hopeless burden for everyone. In the back of everyone's mind will be thoughts of what caused this to happen, including 'Am I to blame?', 'What did I do wrong?' and 'Will they get better?' or 'What will the neighbours or relatives say?' In these cases, you may get a conflict producing a conspiracy of silence, in which everyone suffers to some degree. On visiting the sufferer, the family members will be looking for signs of improvement. They will also place themselves under enormous pressure to be cheerful and to find positive things to say. Because the sufferer may be in hospital for several weeks or even months, this can be an emotional drain on all family members. Hopefully, by this stage, the family will start to obtain information from the hospital staff, self-help groups or the local library. In any illness, but particularly in schizophrenia, information is empowering. Knowing what is happening and how it is treated is the first step to retaking charge of as near as normal family life as possible. Should this not happen, problems within the family may start to appear, such as marital disharmony, or, for younger family members, problems in school.

Firstly, when visiting a person with schizophrenia in hospital don't feel you have to entertain them. It is not a realistic goal. Besides, patients themselves may not be communicating as before and some may even appear dishevelled. Do try to alleviate the stress on other visitors by talking about normal family events and happenings. This can dissipate the pressure of everyone silently conspiring to be cheerful when they obviously need to continue their own normal lives. Do not try and visit your relative every day. This just makes other family members and friends feel guilty that they cannot rearrange their lives in this superhuman fashion. A hospital visiting rota, where people take turns at visiting, keeps everyone fresh. Some families insist that all members participate in the rota. However, care needs to be taken in regard to emotionally blackmailing people into visiting. Everyone has their own fears regarding mental health. Some people, however unrealistic, may have fears about catching the illness or being attacked in the ward. Others may just not be able to cope with a hospital setting, which reminds them of their own vulnerability and mortality.

It is always essential to communicate as a family. Meetings at which all members are encouraged and allowed to express and discuss their fears, can overcome difficulties. Otherwise, petty worries remain unleashed and will probably fester into major anxieties. It is essential for the family to maintain their own social lives. All the energy and conversation in the home must not be allowed to be dominated by the plight of the sick person. In families where this is allowed to happen, normal visitors to the home may stop visiting. Once again, this cuts off outside contacts who would normally bring in different topics of conversation. Family members must continue with evening or weekend activities. Not only will this provide an outlet for stress, but it will also enable the hospital visitor to keep the sufferer up-to-date with the outside world. Should concerns arise when visiting the sufferer in hospital, discuss these with the appropriate ward staff immediately. If concerns are not addressed at this stage, they can be quickly magnified into major problems. What started out as small concerns can multiply into major causes of stress and cause emotional distress for many family members back home. By keeping up-to-date with the progress of the sufferer and arming yourself with information, the family can cope with the major trauma of a prolonged hospital stay.

After the first admission to hospital, discharge is the next highly stressful period for families. Firstly, they have to accept that their relative is not returning home 'cured' but rather with their symptoms controlled, and that the road back to health and a quality life is just beginning. This often means that, on return home, a period in a rehabilitation centre is recommended. Sufferers will often misinterpret the need for rehabilitation and refuse to attend, instead choosing to spend long periods of time in bed isolated from their families. This lack of motivation and interaction puts a huge burden on the family's ability to cope.

Many sufferers have a very poor sense of their own history and will continue making the same mistakes, e.g. going off their medications or continuing to try to achieve what they would have expected to achieve before the onset of the illness. Thus, families experience ongoing renewed stress and loss as they await the next relapse and feel hopeless in preventing it. An analogous situation is how a wife copes when she knows that her husband has been killed in action as opposed to when she has been informed that he is missing in action. Because it is an illness so dependent on ongoing observation, the likely outcome for each sufferer cannot be accurately predicted and each case finds its own course. Thus, relatives can still be dealing with the unknown many years after a diagnosis is made.

Parents also have the ongoing stress and anxiety of meeting the needs of their other children as well as being responsive to those of the sufferer's. Parents often have to come to terms with the fact that the other siblings resent the one who is ill and may feel embarrassed by his social behaviour and therefore stop bringing friends to the house. Thus, parents often must stop following their instincts as much as possible for their sick child, and allow the sufferer to attain his own level of coping as soon as possible after the illness is diagnosed. Parents who have become total carers often wonder, 'What will happen when I'm gone', if they have not achieved appropriate independence for themselves and their sufferer as they face their own old age.

A lot of people who have been diagnosed with schizophrenia attempt suicide and many are successful. Because of the stigma which exists about suicide and the religious connotations it still has in our society, one of the most stressful things which families have to face is that they cannot prevent deliberate self-harm and that they must respond to every crisis involving their sufferer in a manner so as to prevent suicide. This can conversely be used by the sufferer as a means of blackmailing his relatives, and can in the long-run be very detrimental to the sufferer taking responsibility for his illness and finding his own level in society. It must never be forgotten by professionals, however, that every suicide attempt is guilt-inducing and shattering for families and that they need a forum in which to ventilate their feelings of inadequacy, hopelessness and even anger at the sufferer, for what they are being forced to endure.

It is essential for the family to realise that they cannot live the sufferers' lives for them. Nor, through any amount of effort, can they give the sufferer back the quality of life previously expected. Therefore, families must allow the sufferer to find their own place within society. In order to achieve this, families have to offer, whenever possible, age-appropriate care. Although professional carers can provide guidance, the best way of providing ongoing support is to join a self-help group. Talking to people who have experienced similar problems helps share the burden and can generate original solutions. If there is an education course regarding schizophrenia in the locality, several members of the family may benefit. Although there are no definite rights and wrongs, if all the family have the same information and insights, family conflicts regarding future plans are more manageable.

Where sufferers cannot cope with living on their own, a residential rehabilitation hostel may be the most appropriate course of action. Families must not fall into the trap of seeing themselves as failures if this is recommended. Rather, they should look at this option by asking themselves, 'Will a period in a supervised hostel help my son, daughter, brother, sister physically and emotionally to cope better with independent living?' The achievement of a sufferer in terms of having an optimum lifestyle and being able to manage their own illness is very reassuring for other family members. Unfortunately, not everyone with schizophrenia has this option and some remain at home for lengthy periods.

In teaching families the special skills required to cope with schizophrenia, it is essential to remember that even when both they and the sufferer are doing all the right things to manage the illness, there is still the possibility of relapse. Therefore, families must realise the extra pressure they are under with this ongoing work which needs to be done to improve the sufferers subjective feeling regarding their quality of life and their feelings of self-worth.

Developments in understanding the causes and treatment of schizophrenia are gaining ground. Psychiatrists and research organisations are focusing on this potentially very debilitating and expensive illness to find a cure. In the meantime, sufferers, relatives and healthcare professionals must work together to explode myths, push for the provision of quality services and ensure that those affected by schizophrenia are afforded the dignity of having a useful place in society.

For sufferers, this means having to take medication to control the illness and coming to terms with the facts regarding staying well. For relatives, this means allowing the sufferer to find their own place in society and finding healthcare professionals who are informed and caring. For healthcare professionals, it means having to continually evaluate available services for their effectiveness in relieving sufferers and their families.

14

Stress and Old Age

by

Dr Margo Wrigley

Stress is the modern plague. Everyone complains of it – children at school under exam pressure, working mothers, men on short-term work contracts. Many look forward to retirement, seeing it as a long-awaited time of relaxation and so it is for most people. However, some old people are prey to stress and suffer greatly. Crippling poor self-esteem may result in older people feeling they have no role in society and are without value. This chapter will examine what causes stress in older people; who is vulnerable; how it affects older people and how to deal with it.

One of the major causes of stress in old age is the many *losses* which may occur. These include loss of occupation both paid or in the home; loss of family, friends or spouse through death; loss of one's own health; loss of income and loss of sensory faculties (poor sight and hearing). Often, a number of these losses are present, thereby exacerbating stress.

Another major cause of stress in old age is the feeling of *personal helplessness* which is particularly likely to occur in people who are in residential care. Rather surprisingly, children can continue to cause stress and in some ways perhaps be more of a stress because the older parent may watch them making mistakes whilst no longer having any control over what they do.

Very often, problems affecting an older person's children which they feel helpless to do anything about cause great stress — for instance, a marital separation and drug or alcohol abuse. Quite often, elderly people feel a sense of helplessness about what is going on around them. For instance, many elderly people have been much distressed by drug-dealing which they feel they can do little to change.

Generally, being over-involved and judgmental are counter-productive. What seems to be most helpful is to try and maintain contact and this is particularly important where there are grand-children who may be caught up in the conflict. An important part of all of this is for older people to accept that their children are now adults and are responsible for their own actions.

To prevent stress in later life it is necessary to maintain good health, as far as possible. This depends on the intake of a proper diet. Physical vulnerability can lead to stress in some older people. Very simple problems like falls (if a person is a little unsafe on their feet) or more serious incidents such as muggings, which are much more prevalent nowadays, and can lead to great stress and fear.

Finally, *sensory impairments* such as hearing or visual loss make people vulnerable to stress: visual problems because they sap confidence to go out and about and deafness because it contributes to social isolation at an interpersonal level.

Dementia is a condition which is more common in old age. It affects 1 in 20 people over the age of 65, and this increases to 1 in 5 of those over the age of 80. In the early stages of dementia, when people may realise that their memories are fading, they may become extremely stressed. This can manifest itself as either *Anxiety* or *Depression*.

It is important to recognise and treat these stress-related disorders because they can lead to functional decompensation. What this means is that the person becomes more confused as a consequence of having a superimposed anxiety or depression and this makes them more dependent on help. Recognition and treatment of the anxiety and depression means that the level of function is likely to improve. This might make all the difference between a person being able to stay at home rather than having to move into residential care. Paranoid symptoms can develop in those with dementia, especially people who were loners and inclined to be suspicious.

For some elderly people, old age brings an unexpected caring role if their spouse or perhaps a sibling develops dementia or severe physical dependency. The demands of such a role often cause great stress.

The effects of stress in *Carers* are legion and will obviously include carers developing anxiety or depression. However, some also feel guilty, believing they are not doing enough for their dependent relative or they are not coping. Very occasionally, carers become so stressed that they start to neglect their dependent relative or show anger towards them. This is obviously a worrying situation for both the carer and the dependent person, and needs to be recognised so that help can be offered to both parties.

The role of carer often creeps up on a person until they are too busy or too exhausted to look for the help that they need. The public health nurse and GP are the access points to the health and social services required by carers and their dependent relative. These should be contacted early on to make sure that stress does not become unmanageable. Other useful contact points are the Carers' Association as well as other agencies such as the Alzheimer's Society of Ireland, AWARE, which deals with depression, and the Mental Health Association of Ireland. The latter three groups provide specific support for carers who have relatives with various mental health problems. In addition, the Alzheimer's Society also provides day and overnight respite care. The point cannot be too strongly made that carers should not be afraid to ask for help nor, indeed, feel ashamed of asking for help. If they are free from stress, as far as this is possible, it will not only benefit them but also the person for whom they are caring.

Abuse of elderly people by their kin is increasingly recognised as a problem, much as child abuse was some years ago. The abuse can be physical, mental, sexual or financial and causes extreme stress and distress for the elderly person involved. Such a person may find themselves upset by the abuse, completely at sea with regard to seeking help and, indeed, reluctant to look for help because of misguided loyalty to their abusive relative.There is a myth that elderly abuse only effects older people who are too confused to report it. People who are physically dependent are also subject to this, as well as older people who have neither mental or physical problems. The abused person is often too frightened or too ashamed to complain about what is happening for fear that they may be put into a nursing home or because they may feel that they are letting down a relative. This is largely why the problem is so very difficult to manage.

The first step is that the abused person should talk to a trusted relative or, indeed, their public health nurse or their family doctor. If the person is very well otherwise, support may then be all that is needed to help the person face up to the abuser, but in some situations it may be essential that legal advice is sought from a solicitor with regard to barring or protection orders.

Where a person is physically dependent it may be possible for the older person to stay in their own house with support services but if they are very severely impaired this may not be the best option. However, because they do not have a mental health problem impairing mental competence they may be able to take legal action such as protection orders or ensure that proper legal provisions have been put in place by making a will and drawing up an enduring power of attorney.

Those who suffer from dementia and are being abused are currently dealt with using the 'best interest' principle. This involves a full assessment (as it does in the other two situations) on the basis of which a decision is made as to how the person can be best helped. New mental health legislation will include a provision for a Care Order which will be very like the Safety Order which is now available for children who are being abused. It will then be possible to move a person with dementia who is being abused to a place of safety, such as a nursing home, on foot of a Court Order which will also stipulate to whom access may be given. This will mean that the person who is abusing them can be barred. If the person with dementia has substantial assets it will still be necessary for them to be made a Ward of Court to ensure that they are not exploited and that proper provision can be made for their care.

There are undoubtedly certain *personality types* who are more prone to stress when they grow old. These include those who have always had low self-esteem and who find the vicissitudes of old age particularly difficult to tolerate. Also, those who are socially retiring and who have depended on their occupation or their role as parents to prop up their self-esteem and enhance their social interactiveness are prone to stress in old age. Those who haven't developed any social interests before retirement can feel lost without employment or family to keep them busy. Hand in hand with this, is the particular vulnerability of those without a confidante. The old adage 'a trouble shared is a trouble halved' certainly applies in old age and research has shown that those who lack such a confiding relationship are susceptible to developing depression in later life.

Older people who have always had difficulty coping with stress, will obviously find old age a challenge and a time when they are likely to continue to have problems. Paradoxically, overly independent people also run into trouble in old age. If they develop physical problems which mean that they need to avail of social services or medical attention they are reluctant to accept this and put themselves under enormous stress by struggling to manage alone rather than accept the help that is available for them.

People who have never developed any hobbies or interests run into enormous troubles in old age. Quite often they have enjoyed being very busy in their job or with their family and so they find the lack of occupation in old age extremely stressful.

Stress in old age can manifest itself in many ways. The most obvious manifestation is of an *Anxiety State*. This is characterised by feelings of anxiousness and fear which the person often cannot explain. Quite often it is associated with physical symptoms of anxiety such as palpitations, shortness of breath, sweating, stomach pains and headaches which may lead the person to believe they have a physical problem and so seek help for that rather than for the psychological distress which is causing the physical symptoms.

Depression is a very common result of stress in old age. It affects between 10–15% of elderly people, and is more common in women. It can be severe in about 1% of cases. Some people will be aware of feeling depressed and miserable. They may or may not be able to attribute it to certain circumstances or events in their life. Characteristic features of depression are that the person often feels hopeless about their future; may at times wish they were dead; and indeed, in the most severe cases, successful suicide may occur. Often, people with depression are beset with thoughts of guilt and self-blame which are exaggerated or unfounded. For instance, they may blame themselves for an incident that occurred many years ago which they have blown out of proportion. Physical symptoms are also part of depression. Typically, these include loss of appetite, loss of interest in appearance, home or family and disturbed sleep periods. Often, the person will wake early and brood about the hopelessness of their life. Usually, people describe themselves as feeling worst in the mornings. Up to 50% of elderly people do not actually use the term depression to describe how they feel when they are clinically depressed. This is because older people often do not consider it respectable to complain of a psychological problem and hence their inclination is to latch onto physical ill-health as a cause of their state. The stigma of mental illness still persists, particularly for older people.

Specialist old-age psychiatry services usually see people in their own home. Others offer an outpatient appointment in a local health centre or a general hospital. A wide range of helpful measures can be provided by the psychiatric services, including special programmes which deal with problems such as low self-esteem. Such programmes usually take place in day hospitals. Admission to hospital is only considered as a last resort for those who are very severely depressed. The outlook for depression is very good provided it is treated promptly and energetically. It is also essential that any precipitating and maintaining factors are identified and attended to in order to ensure that the condition does not reoccur. In all of this it is important that the depressed person plays as active a part as possible in their treatment. This will further improve the outcome.

It is not unusual for an older person, after a fall or a mugging, to develop anxiety symptoms which crystallise into a *phobia*. The most common phobia is *Agoraphobia*, the fear of going out. A typical scenario is of an elderly person who has tripped over a pavement and who then develops a fear of falling when they are out. They, therefore, gradually stop going out and eventually become housebound. In the end, the actual thought of going out brings on all the symptoms of anxiety, which include palpitations, shakiness, shortness of breath, etc., making them quite convinced that they are likely to fall and so a vicious cycle develops with the person becoming confined to the home. This sort of behaviour is quite easily attributed by everyone else just to old age. The person may feel ashamed of describing how they are feeling or, indeed, believe that this is just part of the ageing process and so they continue to remain housebound.

Phobias, particularly Agoraphobia, are very easily missed in an elderly person because the tendency to confine oneself to the home is facilitated by support services such as Meals on Wheels. There is then no real need for the person to go out. In these cases the public health nurse is usually involved with the person and it is important that if the nurse has not recognised what is going on that a relative or friend tips the nurse off so that specialised help can be obtained. Usually, treatment requires referral by the GP to the local psychiatric service. A home assessment is then undertaken and a programme is carried out by a psychologist, an occupational therapist or a behaviour therapist nurse which is based on the gradual exposure of the older person to the feared situation so that they regain confidence about going out again. This is done extremely slowly and with a lot of support and works extremely well for most people. Again, its success depends upon the older person being motivated to participate in the programme.

Occasionally, an elderly person under stress will escape from it by adopting the *sick role*. They become hypochondriacal, that is pre–occupied with various physical symptoms leading to dependence on those around them. This dependence means that they do not have to face up to the stresses in their life and, of course, it is an acceptable way of doing so since old age and being sick are firmly linked together in the minds of most people.

Sometimes, an older person under stress can become paranoid. This is likely to occur in those who have overly-independent personalities who then fall prey to physical ill-health in older age. They are obviously stressed by their ill-health and need to accept help but are reluctant to do so. In their minds they are fighting against becoming dependent. This idea may manifest itself as *Paranoia* in which all offers of help by friends and relatives as well as services are viewed suspiciously. Some become actively hostile towards people who offer help and make abusive remarks. Sometimes, delusions or false ideas about people develop and relatives are accused of just being interested in them to get their money or even of taking their money. It can be quite difficult to tease out what the real situation is because sudden concern by relatives in an elderly person may well be precipitated by self-interest rather than by altruism and abuse may occur.

Some mention has already been made of people who are developing *Dementia*. In the early stages, retaining insight into their memory problems may cause an anxiety state or a depressive illness.

It is well-recognised that a small number of elderly people (especially women) who are lonely and stressed may steal items from shops which they do not need at all. This behaviour seems to be the manifestation of their stress. It is referred to as *Kleptomania*: 'A madness for stealing'.

Finally, *Alcohol Abuse*, starting in later life, is increasingly recognised as a problem. It tends to occur in isolated, lonely women who turn to drink to ward off their feelings of isolation and low self-esteem. Alcohol is now much more easily available in respectable places such as off-licences and supermarkets and, therefore, is accessible to this at-risk group. Usually, the drinking is done very secretly and it is some time before it comes to the attention of family or the health services because of poor physical health, the tendency to fall, malnutrition, confusion or depression.

Alcohol Abuse requires help from the General Practitioner who may try, if the person is not drinking too heavily, to detoxify or get the person off alcohol at home and then involve the public health nurse and other support services in encouraging the person to partake in local group activities. However, if drinking has been very heavy or the person is quite debilitated by their intake of alcohol, then psychiatric assessment and admission for detoxification is usually advised and a programme of rehabilitation is subsequently instituted which treats alcoholism from two aspects. The first challenge is to help the person recognise and acknowledge that they have an alcohol problem and what that is doing to them, and the second aspect of the programme is to encourage the person to develop interests and activities locally since it is usually isolation that has precipitated the problem in the first place. This quite often involves attendance at the local day hospital to help the person regain their self-confidence and to enable them to join in social events.

The best protection against stress in old age is to make sure that interests are developed. These should be real interests which ideally also encourage socialising and which have developed long before old age is reached. It is far too late to think of developing such interests the day after you retire. This means that those who are more rounded individuals with a lifestyle which encompasses work, home and a number of interests will enjoy old age. Many firms now offer pre-retirement courses which are useful but need to be offered a couple of years before retirement age so that people have time to plan, particularly for the social aspects of retirement. Financial worries can be very weighty in old age, so it is important that people early in their working life make provision for themselves through pension schemes and from middle-age onwards put their affairs in order, in terms of making a will and drawing up an enduring power of attorney.

It has long been recognised that there is an increased level of stress resulting in depression amongst older people in residential care. There are a number of obvious reasons for this such as the stress of moving into care, the physical dependency which has precipitated this move and, very occasionally, the care practices within the home. Very often, after allowing for an adjustment period for settling in, the depression resolves. Depression can be prevented by ensuring that there are good care practices within the home which include suitable activities and sensible routines. However, sometimes the care practices themselves are such that they are largely responsible for depression occurring. A vulnerable elderly resident may be afraid to explain why they feel so miserable in case they are thrown out of the home and the worry and distress caused by this leads to depression. The best approach is for the resident to complain – making a reasonable case with the support of their family. If this is unsuccessful and the person continues to be unhappy and depressed in a poorly-run home, then they should consider moving to another home. People with dementia in residential care may also suffer from depression but may be incapable of describing how they feel.

A vigilant family is important, as well as vigilant nursing home staff. The family can be helpful in noticing a contrast between how the person was at home, in terms of their mood, and how they are in the nursing home. Allowance does, of course, have to be made for the person to settle into the nursing home over a period of weeks. To prevent these problems occurring, families must be careful when choosing a nursing home. If it is possible, involve the elderly person in the decision. Otherwise, the family should make sure that they look at the nursing home very carefully, discuss the routine and care practices with the person in charge of the home and also see whether the residents look happy and contented in the home. Finally, there is statutory control in the form of inspection of nursing homes under the auspicies of the Nursing Home Act, which ensures that standards are maintained.

Whilst Ireland, compared to other countries, has a good record in terms of providing good pensions and good ancillary supports such as free travel and free TV licences for its older citizens, nevertheless, some people do find themselves under stress because of penury. In the first instance, contact the public health nurse for information about social welfare entitlements and how to access them. An increasingly common situation that older people find themselves in is being income-poor but asset-rich. In other words, they may have a house which is very valuable but still have a very poor income. Consideration should be given to mobilising income from the home by selling the house, buying a smaller place and investing the income. Good, independent legal and financial advice are essential if contemplating such a step.

This chapter has focused on stress in old age and may, therefore, give a misleading picture of old age as a terrible time beset by misery, poverty, isolation and dependency. This is far from the case. The majority of older people find this time of life one of great joy, now that they are relieved from the many burdens of care concerned with working and rearing children. They now have time to reflect and consolidate. A good example of this is the pleasure many older people get from their grandchildren, whereas their enjoyment of their own children was tempered by obligations of care, education and discipline.

What about the person who has succumbed to stress already? Any such person should seek help. The help sought depends obviously on the nature and severity of the problem. As a general principle, those who have close relationships with relatives or a confiding friend will often be helped by discussing matters with these people first. Quite often, this may be enough to sort out the problem. Sometimes, assistance from health and welfare services may be needed and, in the first instance, a public health nurse or the person's General Practitioner should be contacted.

A very important message coming from this chapter is that everyone should be preparing throughout adulthood to ensure that their old age is rewarding by developing interests and making time to socialise. Very often these two aspects are linked. Part of this preparation should be to ensure that financial and legal provisions for old age are made.

For those who do run into trouble, many problems can be helped by discussion with friends and family and by adopting a positive mind-frame to going out and about again. Equally, simple measures can help those under stress who are housebound or in residential care. More engrained or complicated problems can be helped by the family doctor, with some requiring referral to the psychiatric services.

Voluntary organisations cannot be underestimated in the help they provide. This is often very much more acceptable to people since they then receive support from people who find themselves in similar situations, for instance carers of those with dementia.

So, even for those who are troubled by stress, help is available and should be sought. The vast majority of difficulties can be dealt with, resulting in an improvement in the quality of life for the older person.

15

Stress Control and You

by

Tom Moriarty

Just imagine that you wish to walk across a busy road. What is the first thing you do? You stand on the footpath, look left and right, come to the conclusion that it is not yet time to walk across because the traffic is heavy in both directions. When you see the cars and trucks whizzing past, you experience some stress which gives you the message that it is not yet safe to cross this busy roadway. After some minutes a break comes in the traffic, you look left and right and see that it is now safe to walk across. You then proceed to step onto the roadway but you constantly keep looking left and right because you still have some anxiety and concerns about possible oncoming traffic. When you are halfway across this road you look to your right and you see a large articulated truck speeding towards you. You immediately experience significant stress, come to the conclusion that you are in danger, so you immediately dash to the other side of the road for safety. Does this scene make sense? Damn right it does!

Let us consider for a moment what is taking place in the above scene. You are standing on the footpath and notice traffic travelling in both directions. You experience some stress regarding the obvious dangers of crossing at this point in time. This stress ensures your safety. As soon as the stress subsides, you take a decision that it is now safe to cross and you proceed to implement this decision. However, halfway across the road, you again experience some significant stress when you notice the large truck approaching you. This stress stimulates you to take action; and you rush to the other side of the road, reach the safety of the footpath and again your stress subsides.

Most people regard stress as a negative and destructive experience. However, when you were crossing the road, stress ensured your survival! Thus, the experience of stress in that particular situation was both positive and constructive. Stress is necessary for survival and everybody experiences stress. Thus, the notion that stress is always negative is a fallacy. We all need to experience an optimal level of stress in order to cope effectively with potentially problematic situations. Stress is only problematic when it is excessive. Stress occurs when you perceive the demands of a particular situation to be greater than your capacity or resources to deal with that situation. However, your conclusion about your inability to cope with the situation may not be very accurate. Most people who refer to themselves as 'stressed' believe that they do not have the capacity to deal with their stress and see control as being totally outside themselves. This inaccurate perception inevitably increases the individual's stress levels. Most people who experience excessive stress do not really understand that they have a way out of it and that they can do a lot to help themselves.

How can you help yourself to manage your own stress? Before you start thinking about practical strategies to deal with stress you should first *educate* yourself regarding the concept. Lack of knowledge about the concept can be stressful, in itself. There is a vast range of information available today on the subject of stress. An increasing number of adult education courses include this topic in their curricula, while a number of specialist training services provide comprehensive training programmes. There is also a large range of literature available in most reputable bookstores. As you begin to gain more knowledge regarding the causes and outcomes of stress you should begin to appreciate that its control is well within your grasp. In this context, a little knowledge is extremely helpful.

Your next step is to make the decision that you will take charge of your own stress rather than giving that responsibility to others. It is important to understand that only you can solve your problems. The role of key people in your life is to facilitate you in this process. However, in order to make such a critical decision you must first ensure that your levels of *self-esteem* are sufficient and adequate. But what is self-esteem you may well ask? Self-esteem is the degree to which you feel positive about yourself. A predominant characteristic of people who regard themselves as 'stressed' is that they present with very low self-esteem. In essence, they are not very nice to themselves. High self-esteem gives you the strength to make and implement difficult decisions such as taking charge of your stress.

So how do you improve your own levels of self-esteem? Very simply, start saying nice things to yourself, about yourself, rather than hoping other people will do it for you. For example, when you have completed a particular task to your satisfaction, don't just walk away from it; stop for a few moments, think about how well you have completed that particular task and say to yourself, 'I did that job really well and I obviously have a lot of ability'. It is essential that you start giving yourself credit, where credit is due. Don't be embarrassed or uneasy about this. Remember, nobody can hear you! Complimenting yourself on your practical achievements enhances your self-esteem.

Another practical way of achieving this is to keep a daily written record of your achievements. This task should be completed at the end of each day and should focus on all your successful activities during that particular day; record every achievement, no matter how small it has been. When you have completed this task make yourself comfortable, close your eyes and think again about your achievements on that particular day. This is the process of esteeming yourself. If you discipline yourself to complete this task at the end of each day, your levels of self-esteem will gradually improve, you will become more self-confident and self-assured and your capacity to cope with stress and develop effective problem-solving strategies will be enhanced. The thrust of this strategy is to facilitate you to take charge of your own self-esteem and ultimately take charge of your own stress.

An extension of this strategy is to develop a list of life achievements pertaining to all aspects of your life to date. When you have completed this task you should take time out for approximately five minutes each day, choose one life achievement, close your eyes and relive that particular experience. Once again, you will be esteeming yourself. People who are stressed are people who have lost touch with the positive aspects of their lives, including previously effective coping skills. These strategies are practical ways of facilitating you to get back in touch with your positive self.

At the outset, we noted that everyone encounters stress on a daily basis and that stress is essential for survival. How we interpret a potentially stressful situation and, more importantly, how we interpret our capacity to cope with it are critical factors. You probably have the capacity to deal with many so-called stressful situations but because of a significant lack of belief in yourself regarding this issue you invariably tend to misinterpret what is happening. Many people who are experiencing significant stress tend to have a very pessimistic explanatory style which results in somewhat catastrophic conclusions about relatively insignificant comments and events. In dealing with such situations, do not automatically accept your initial conclusion about what is happening or that you do not have the capacity to cope; think again and ask yourself, 'Is my interpretation of the situation correct?' When you reflect you may come to the conclusion that your initial interpretation was inaccurate and that you have dealt successfully with this or a similar situation in the past. This is a further key strategy in dealing with stress. You must discipline yourself to stand back from the situation and reappraise it, reflect how you have dealt successfully with similar situations in the past and transfer those particular strategies to the present. This will gradually happen if you are diligent in the process of esteeming yourself as previously outlined; the process of esteeming yourself puts you back in touch with your previously positive and effective self.

As you rediscover your ability to interpret situations accurately and cope more effectively you should then begin to *prioritise* tasks. Identify tasks which can be dealt with at a later date and only deal today with the situations which require your immediate attention. Also, begin to practice the art of delegation! Take control of the demands being placed upon you, learn to say 'no' to situations which are not your responsibility, identify a proper timescale for tasks and tackle only one situation at a time.

Because many of us regard the experience of stress as a sign of weakness, we tend to secretise the issue. This process of *secretisation* effectively removes one important stress management strategy – talking to others about your stress. It is very important for you to desecretise your stress and seek the support of significant people in your life. The process of talking will relieve a lot of the emotion around your stress and will also put you in touch with how other people have effectively dealt with similar situations. Perhaps present day society tends not to facilitate this process. We may not talk to each other as much as previous generations did. No doubt the advent of modern communication technology has placed us in an essentially passive role with regard to communication. The demise of the extended family and the natural support systems provided therein is another significant loss to our present society. Nevertheless, there are still many opportunities for you to talk to key people in your life and to learn from their experiences.

Let us now focus on how *exercise* can be a very valuable resource in dealing with stress. It is important, in this context, to make a clear distinction between exercise and competitive sport. Exercise is habitual, non-competitive physical activity while competitive sport entails competition against others to prove who is best! Activities include walking, jogging, cycling, swimming, aerobic exercises, bowling, golf, tennis, etc. Such activities can be on an individual basis or a team basis. Although the belief that physical activity can be beneficial for psychological health is not new, there has been a great deal of recent research on the positive link between exercise and psychological health. The International Society of Sport Psychology stated, in 1992, that exercise is associated with a reduction in anxiety levels, reductions in mild to moderate depression, increased capacity to cope with stress and has beneficial emotional effects across all ages and in both sexes. It facilitates the relief of muscle tension and increases the body temperature which causes a more relaxed state. Exercise also provides you with a sense of mastery and achievement in a very practical, simple way and will ultimately lead to an improved self-image and body image, a sense of self-worth and enhanced self-esteem.

While most of us agree with these benefits many of us do not engage in regular exercise activity! How much exercise do you take? Do you take exercise on a daily basis? If the answer to either of these questions is 'none' or 'no' then you need to change your lifestyle to include regular daily exercise. Excuses such as lack of time and expense are not really valid. Having a brisk walk, cycling, jogging, swimming, etc. does not involve significant expense and with a little effective time management, can be easily facilitated. It is important also to note that the scientific research to date has indicated that moderate exercise is more beneficial than very intense exercise.

The pace of life in our present society is far more intense than in previous generations. Education and employment are central to all our lives and competitiveness impinges on both. Neither the body nor the mind has a limitless capacity to compete on an indefinite basis. It is essential that we all take time out to relax and recharge our batteries. *Relaxation* does not necessarily have to be an expensive holiday abroad or a weekend away from home. Relaxation can take place on a daily basis without any monetary cost. For example, you can take ten minutes each morning and afternoon to sit back, close your eyes and revisit some very pleasant, relaxing and enjoyable experience you have had in the past. Alternatively, you can listen to some relaxing music or indeed utilise one of the many progressive muscular relaxation techniques currently available on audiotape. Perhaps you could engage in such activity during your coffee breaks and lunch breaks at work. How many stress-free breaks do you take each day? Have you ever considered ensuring that your lunch breaks and coffee breaks are periods when you engage in total relaxation rather than discussing the problems and crises of everyday life with your friends and work colleagues? Those who have planned and implemented such stress-free breaks not alone find them energising and refreshing but also experience a sense of mastery which is vital to the control of stress.

Management of your work stress is now possibly as important as the management of your personal stress and, of course, both can overlap. The range of *stress management* strategies we have already discussed can be equally applied to your work environment. The importance of daily exercise and stress-free breaks become critical with regard to occupational stress. However, you may also have to consider a number of work-related stress management strategies in addition to those we have already discussed. In particular, you may have to improve your time- and task-management. Effective management of your working day can be achieved by making a daily action list, learning to delegate, engaging in disciplined forward planning with realistic goals, preparing properly for meetings, only taking or making telephone calls that are necessary and learning to say *no*. In a very competitive and pressurised work environment it is very easy to ignore or minimise your achievements and become hypersensitive to criticisms and difficulties. In order to effectively manage this potentially dangerous dynamic you should seriously consider keeping a work diary in which you record your daily achievements. At the end of each week, you should read this record of achievements; this strategy will keep you in touch with your positive workself and counteract the human tendency only to recall problematic work issues. You may be extremely reluctant and indeed embarrassed to engage in self-praise. Remember, it is essential for the management of stress that you keep in touch with your positive self. This strategy is both personal and private and for your eyes only. Don't be afraid to give yourself credit where credit is due!

A final stress management strategy is to set yourself *realistic targets* and *goals*. You may impose an inordinately high stress level on yourself by having unrealistic expectations of what you can achieve. When you set yourself a target or goal, stop for a moment and ask yourself, 'Is it realistic for me to achieve this?' In attempting to answer this question you must look at the practical obstacles you will encounter in attempting to achieve your goal and also identify strategies to overcome those obstacles. Most of us fail to achieve our goals either because they are unrealistic or because we have failed to identify the obstacles we are likely to encounter in attempting to achieve them. We may be quite impulsive and somewhat idealistic in our goal-setting techniques. If this applies to you change it immediately!

The purpose of this chapter is to give you some practical strategies for dealing with stress. The thrust of these strategies is to facilitate you to take charge and take ownership of your own stress rather than relying on others to make life more pleasant for you. Perhaps a summary of the key points would be helpful:

- Educate yourself regarding the concept of stress.
- Recognise your own stress and understand it.
- Decide to do something about it.
- Think positively about your abilities, past and present.
- Recognise and acknowledge your daily achievements.
- Set realistic goals for yourself, identify the obstacles you are likely to encounter in trying to achieve these goals and identify a strategy for overcoming these obstacles.
- Talk to others about your stress and utilise available social support.
- Engage in daily exercise.
- Learn how to release muscular tension before it builds up.
- Create daily relaxation periods.
- Do not misinterpret situations or underestimate your ability to cope.
- Make more active use of breaks during your working day.

- Learn to prioritise, delegate and say *no*.
- Improve your time management.

There is no doubt that you can be far more effective in the way you deal with stress, providing you make the decision to do something about it. Take courage from the fact that others who have made this decision have been extremely successful in coping. Take courage also from the fact that you have previously been successful in coping with many stressful situations. Think positively about your abilities, pay attention to your physical well-being, use available social support, set realistic goals for yourself and you too will be successful.